PROJECT Z

ZOMBIES ARE PEOPLE, TOO

Text copyright © 2019 by Tommy Greenwald
Illustrations by Dave Bardin © 2019 Scholastic Inc.

ISBN 978-1-338-30596-8

10 9 8 7 6 5 4 3 2 1   19 20 21 22 23

Printed in the U.S.A. 40

First printing 2019

Book design by Yaffa Jaskoll

PROJECT Z
ZOMBIES ARE PEOPLE, TOO

TOMMY GREENWALD

SCHOLASTIC INC.

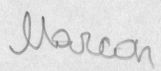

There's no such thing as fitting in.
Only fitting in your own skin.

A ZOMBIE GLOSSARY:

GOVERNMENT TERRITORY 278 (OTHERWISE KNOWN AS THE TERRITORY): THE SECRET LAB WHERE ZOMBIES WERE FIRST DEVELOPED

NORBUS CLACKNOZZLE: GOVERNMENT-ISSUED NAME OF ARNOLD Z. OMBEE

THE ZOMBIE ZING: A WAY ZOMBIES CAN TEMPORARILY PARALYZE HUMANS BY PINCHING THEM ON THE SHOULDER

THE SALT MELT: A WAY HUMANS CAN TEMPORARILY PARALYZE ZOMBIES BY POURING SALT OVER THEM

JELLY BEANS: THE ONLY THING ZOMBIES CAN EAT

170: THE AVERAGE IQ OF A ZOMBIE (IN OTHER WORDS, THEY'RE VERY SMART)

THE RED STREAK: A MARK THAT SCIENTISTS PLACED ACROSS THE PUPILS OF ZOMBIES, AS A MEANS OF IDENTIFYING THEM

ORANGE JUMPSUIT: THE OFFICIAL UNIFORM OF ZOMBIES

MEMORY: SOMETHING ZOMBIES HAVE VERY LITTLE OF

SLEEPING, BREATHING, LIVING: THINGS A ZOMBIE DOESN'T DO

Wednesday
May 19, 2027
GT 278
PROJECT Z
THE OUTER BRANCH
ARIZONA

ATTENTION ALL STAFF:

On February 25, 2027, there was a breach at Government Territory 278 at 04:28 hours. Six subjects escaped. Five were immediately captured. The sixth, Subject 48356, code-named Norbus Clacknozzle, has remained at large until now.

We are pleased to report that identification and placement of the sixth subject has finally been confirmed.

Satellite drones have established that Subject 48356 is currently living with a family and being passed off as a human elementary school student. The family has thus far been successful in keeping their arrangement confidential, with the full cooperation of the community.

The mother of the family is Dr. Jennifer Kinder, former medical director of this program. We have every reason to believe she helped organize the initial escape, is now an adversary of the program she helped create, and may be a threat to its very existence.

Plans are being put in place to neutralize this threat. We will be in further communication as those plans get solidified and readied to implement.

JONATHAN JENSEN
Regional Commander, National Martial Services

PROLOGUE

Hi, my name is Arnold Z. Ombee.

Kind of.

It's a long story, and if you want the details, you can read them in my first book, *A ZOMBIE ATE MY HOMEWORK*. But if you don't want the details, here's the short version:

I'm a zombie.

I was brought to life (or afterlife) in a secret lab.

I escaped.

I was rescued by the Kinders, a wonderful family.

They decided that for my own protection, I should pretend to be a regular human boy.

I went to school and made some friends.

People found out I was a zombie.

After a big kerfuffle (a great word, in case you don't know it. I have an embarrassingly large vocabulary, which is why *I* know it), I was allowed to stay with the Kinders.

Sounds like a happy ending, right?

Not so fast.

It was more like a crazy beginning.

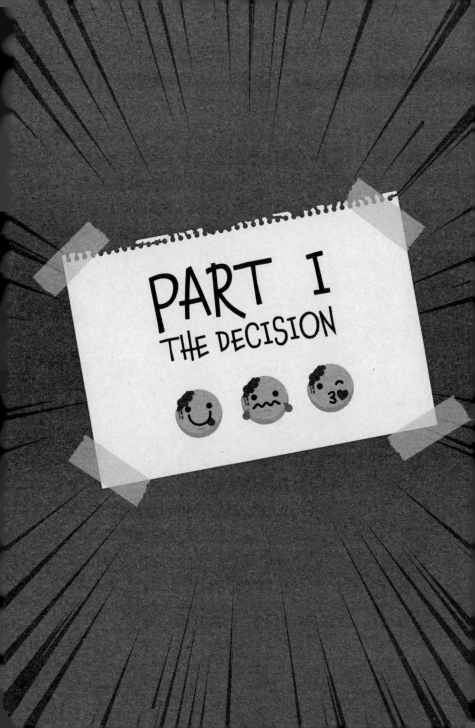

THE SMARTEST KID IN SCHOOL

There's a phrase that used to run through my head all the time back when I first escaped from the lab.

Humans are the enemy. Humans are Dangerous.
Humans are the enemy. Humans are Dangerous.

Jenny Kinder—who is now, unofficially, my mom—said the scientists at the lab programmed those thoughts into my brain so that I would be aggressive toward people.

She would know, since she was one of the scientists. (Long story. Like I said, you can read the first book if you want to know the details.)

Humans are the enemy. Humans are Dangerous.

But guess what? It didn't work. Probably because it's not true.

If they wanted to be accurate, they would have pro-grammed this:

Even though some humans are Dangerous, most aren't. But ALL humans hate homework. Many humans aren't very Good at math. And a significant number of humans would rather Do anything else than pay attention to the teacher.

When I entered the fifth grade at Bernard J. Frumpstein Elementary School, most people treated me like a total outsider—probably because I *was* a total outsider. But there were two people who were nice to me: Evan Brantley, who got on my nerves by flicking the back of my neck on my very first bus ride but quickly became my best pal; and Kiki Ambrose, the most popular kid in the whole school, who decided for some incredibly lucky reason to find me interesting.

At first, all the other kids made fun of me; then, when they saw me temporarily paralyze Ross Klepsaw with the Zombie Zing (it was his fault, I swear), they all got scared of me; and finally, when everyone found out I was a zombie but that I was more interested in being their friend than eating their brains, they accepted me as (almost) one of them.

Which is where the whole tutoring thing comes in.

One day during lunch, a boy named Jimmy Edwards came up to me. I'd barely said five words to him before then, but he slapped me on the back like we were old pals.

"Arnold, buddy boy!" he exclaimed. "How goes it?"

I looked up at him. "It goes it pretty well, how goes it with you?"

"Great, great." Jimmy pulled up a chair next to me. "So yeah, Arnold, I got a little problem, to be honest with you."

"What's that?"

"I'm failing English."

"Oh. Gosh, I'm sorry to hear that."

Kiki, who was sitting on one side of me, rolled her eyes. "Get to the point, Jimmy."

"Right." Jimmy glared at Kiki, then turned back to me. "So anyway, Arnold, I was wondering, since you're so smart and everything, maybe you could, like, help me get my grade up?"

I was confused, since the whole process of school had seemed pretty easy to follow so far. "Help you how? If you do the work the class requires, then surely you will succeed."

Jimmy cleared his throat. "Yeah, well, uh, I guess I haven't exactly done the work required."

"Oh. I understand," I said, even though I didn't.

Evan, who was sitting on the other side of me, saw the confusion on my face. "Here's the thing, Arnold. Not all kids are the same. Some kids do their homework; others don't. Some kids pay attention in class; some kids don't. Some kids like to read; others don't."

"Nobody likes to read," corrected Jimmy.

"That's not true," insisted Evan. "I do, for example."

Jimmy snickered. "No *normal* people."

"Enough, you two," said Kiki. "I love to read, but that doesn't make me any better than kids who don't. We're just different, that's all." She fiddled with her hair. "The point is, Arnold, that you're, like, the smartest kid in the whole school, and Jimmy needs some help. Will you help him?"

"Of course I will."

That day after school, I taught Jimmy the difference between *its* and *it's*, made sure he knew the difference between an adjective and an adverb, and showed him how to use *sluggish* in a sentence ("Eating four ice cream sandwiches at lunch made Timmy sluggish at soccer practice"). Then, for the next week, I helped him with a whole bunch of other stuff.

When Jimmy got an eighty one on the test, he ran over to me. "Yo, dude, we did it!"

"You did it," I told him.

"Nah, *we*!" He lifted me up in the air, which wasn't hard for him to do, since he's very strong and I'm very skinny. "Hey, everyone! Arnold here saved my butt! He's, like, a genius!"

And that's basically how I became the unofficial tutor for the entire fifth grade class at Bernard J. Frumpstein Elementary School.

"How much are you making for all this tutoring?" Evan asked me one day, while we were jumping on his trampoline.

I did a triple somersault, which is easy for me because my legs are like rubber bands. Extremely pale rubber bands. "Making? What do you mean, making?"

"I mean, how much are you charging for your work?"

"I'm not charging anything," I told him. "I'm doing it because they need my help."

Evan's eyes went wide. "Are you *kidding* me right now? You need to be getting paid! Makin' the MOAN-NAY!"

Apparently, there was still a lot I needed to learn about the ways of the humans.

A STRANGE MAN

After I'd been living with Jenny and Bill Kinder for about two months, I was able to do the following activities fairly successfully:

1) Brushing my teeth
2) Taking a shower
3) Tying my shoes
4) Passing as a human

However, I was still having trouble with the following:

1) Listening to loud music
2) Watching television shows about roommates who complain about each other
3) Incredibly heavy school backpacks. What's that about?

4) Anything that had to do with football. I just don't get
   that sport at all.

Lester, however, LOVED football. Did I mention
Lester? He's my fifteen-year-old kind-of-brother. When
the Kinders first rescued me, their son, Lester, treated
me like an alien, probably because I pretty much *was* an
alien. He really didn't like having me around at all. But
then this girl he liked, whose name is Darlene, decided I
was the coolest-looking kid in town, and, sure enough,
Lester and I have gotten along pretty well ever since. But
that didn't mean I liked going to his football games. I
went because Jenny Kinder—who I guess I should start
calling Mom—and Bill Kinder (Dad) didn't really give me
much choice.

"It's important to have family time," explained Mom.
"We all lead such busy lives that we need to stay connected."

I was confused. "How is watching Lester jump on top
of other people, and watching other people jump on top of
Lester, staying connected?"

"It just is," Dad said. My new parents were the nicest
people you'd ever meet, but sometimes they ran out of
patience explaining normal human things to me.

It was about ten weeks after the Kinders rescued me, at a Friday-night spring league football game where Lester was busy getting smushed underneath another pile of people, when I noticed a man in a red jacket talking to my teacher, Mrs. Huggle. Now, normally I wouldn't think it was such a big deal. I see people talking to my teacher all the time, usually kids complaining about a homework assignment, but there was something about this man that made me look twice.

He seemed familiar.

And since I had no long-term memory and very limited short-term memory, *no one* looked familiar.

But he did.

My parents were watching the game closely, so I didn't want to bother them, but Darlene—who was sitting with us even though she thought football was "barbaric"—was staring at her phone. I tapped her on the shoulder. "Excuse me, Darlene, do you see that man down there talking to Mrs. Huggle?"

Darlene looked up at me with one eye. "Stop being so polite. You don't have to say 'Excuse me.' You can just say 'Yo, Darlene.'"

"Okay. Yo, Darlene, do you see that man down there talking to Mrs. Huggle?"

Darlene glanced up for approximately half a second. "The guy with a beard and glasses? Yeah, I see him."

"Do you know him?"

This time she glanced up an extra second. "Don't think so. Why?"

"I don't know. I feel like I've seen him before."

"So?" Darlene asked, which was a perfectly reasonable question.

Something big happened on the field, and the crowd cheered. "Lester just made a long run!" my dad said. "They're down to the twenty-two-yard line!"

"That's amazing," I said. "I love the twenty-two-yard line. It's my favorite yard line."

Dad shook his head and turned his attention back to the game. My mom gave me a little hug. "I know you don't care about football, and that's just fine," she said. "After the game, we'll all go out for ice cream—how's that sound?"

"It sounds great," I said, even though we both knew that they'd all have ice cream and I'd have jelly beans, because that's all I ever had. I couldn't eat anything else, and I'd never be able to. Just like I'd never sleep, and I'd never breathe, and I'd never be a normal human kid. Because I wasn't that, and it didn't do me any good to think I ever would be.

"Mom?"

"Yes, Arnold?"

"Remember when I told you I couldn't remember anything from my time at the Territory?"

"Of course," she answered. "We programmed all subjects to have very limited short-term memory, because it would have made things much more complicated. And then you hit your head when you ran away, which may well have made your memory even worse."

I pointed at the man in the red jacket who was talking to Mrs. Huggle. "Well then, why do I think I remember him?"

My mom looked up, and as soon as she saw the man I was talking about, her whole face changed. It was like she saw a ghost. (Or a zombie.) But she shook her head.

"I'm not sure." And then out of nowhere, she turned to my dad. "Honey? I'm actually not feeling that well, and Arnold is bored as usual. We're going to go home."

My dad looked shocked. "You're leaving? It's not even halftime! And they're about to take the lead!"

"I know, honey, and I can't wait to hear all about it." My mom grabbed my hand. "Let's go, Arnold."

As we made our way out of the bleachers, I looked down at the man one last time. And then, for the first time, he looked at me, nodded, and smiled.

I suddenly knew where I'd seen him before.

And I knew why he was there.

dR. PRiNCiPAL'S OFFiCE

The principal of our school was a woman named Dr. Principal.

I am not making that up.

Everyone seemed to think that was the most hilarious thing in the world, except for Dr. Principal herself. She didn't think it was hilarious at all. "When you make a joke about it that I haven't heard before, then I'll laugh," is what she would say. I can't say that I blame her.

For a couple of days after the football game, my family acted like nothing was wrong. Lester's team won the game 28–16, and we had our usual celebratory dinner of fried chicken and ice cream. (I watched.) I could tell something was off with my mom, and I think she could tell something was off with me. But neither of us said anything about it, almost as if we both wished it away.

Then, on Monday, my parents told me that we were having a meeting in Dr. Principal's office before school.

"What about?" I asked.

"It's nothing bad," said my dad.

When we got there, Dr. Principal and my teacher, Mrs. Huggle, were sitting there.

So was the man from the football game.

"Welcome," said Dr. Principal. "Please sit down."

We did.

She cleared her throat. "Arnold, I received a call on Friday from the state police, stating that they had become aware of an undocumented fugitive attending school here." She nodded in the direction of the stranger. "They had been tipped off by this man, Dr. Sherman Grasmere. So last night, I asked your parents to come in this morning to discuss the matter."

I turned to my parents. "Is this true?"

My mom nodded. "Yes. Dr. Grasmere is a former colleague of mine from the National Laboratory."

I could feel my ears vibrating. "You said you didn't know why I recognized him."

My mom looked at her shoes. "I wasn't being truthful, and I'm sorry."

Dr. Grasmere stood up and extended his hand to me. I shook it. It was warm, of course. All human hands are warm.

"You didn't go by Arnold when I knew you," he said. "So you do remember me?"

I nodded. "I think so."

"I thought you might. Memories are powerful things—no matter how much we might try to manipulate them. And brains tend to have minds of their own." Dr. Grasmere smiled and stroked his short gray beard. "Dr. Kinder and I were partners on Project Z for quite some time, and I'm very proud of what we accomplished."

"Project Z?" asked Mrs. Huggle.

My mom cleared her throat. "That was the code name of the confidential federal program under which we worked," she explained. "Sherman and I co-directed the lab for three years, until I left. I didn't like where the program was headed." She looked at Dr. Grasmere carefully. "Sherman stayed. And I believe he's still there."

"I am," the doctor confirmed. He took out a big red folder and placed it on the table in front of him but didn't open it. "Dr. Kinder referred to Project Z. I think everyone here knows what this top secret program is all about, but just to briefly reiterate, we have been developing a species of afterlife humans."

"You mean zombies," said Dr. Principal.

Dr. Grasmere nodded. "Correct, zombies, although that is not the technical term." He picked up his folder. "The original plan was to develop these afterlife humans into a fighting force that would invade American society, thus necessitating a national military response. The idea was that our increasingly fractured nation could become more united through the historically unifying cause of fighting a common enemy."

"I ended up opposing this plan," said my mom. "That's why I left. And why I tried to help several afterlifes escape. The only one who made it was you." She grabbed my hand, and I squeezed back.

Mrs. Huggle raised her hand, even though she was the teacher. "When the Kinders adopted Arnold, the entire community rallied behind them, and we have all been sworn to secrecy. So I am curious to know how you found Arnold."

Dr. Grasmere shook his head. "That's not something I can discuss right now, and it's not why I'm here. I have no interest in turning anyone in. In fact, I'm here to help."

My dad spoke for the first time. "Help? How?"

Dr. Grasmere picked up his folder. "We have been doing a great deal of research, and we have come to see the validity of Dr. Kinder's thinking. As a result, the original plan to create a common enemy out of the afterlifes is no longer viable." He paused briefly as he looked down at the folder. "We have a new plan in place, which we'd like to implement as soon as possible."

The school bell rang.

Dr. Principal stood up. "Well, saved by the bell, as they say," she said. "As important as this is, it can't be more important than our students attending school. So, Mrs. Huggle and Arnold, you should go ahead to first class. Dr. and Mr. Kinder, perhaps you can stay and discuss this turn of events with our guest. You may use the conference room next to my office, if you wish."

I looked at my parents, who nodded. "Go ahead, Arnold," said my dad. "We'll discuss all this when you get home."

"For now, don't say a word about any of this," added my mom. "We can't trust any outsiders just yet."

Then she looked at Dr. Grasmere. "I'm afraid I have to include you on that list," she added.

SARAH ANNE

I don't think I've told you about my third good friend yet.

Her name is Sarah Anne, and she's a really interesting person. I met her in my first week at school when we sat together on a bench at recess, and she told me how much she loved horses and poetry. But she didn't "tell" me, exactly: She communicates by pointing at letters on a board to spell out the words she wants to say. I'm not sure why, but she just feels more comfortable doing that than talking the way most people talk. There's also a woman, Ms. Frawley, who helps Sarah Anne deal with stuff like eating her lunch and getting to class, because sometimes Sarah Anne gets nervous and scared when she's around a lot of other people. But the funny thing is, even though all that stuff might make you think that Sarah Anne is a very unusual kind of person, when you get to know her, she's a lot like everyone else.

After the meeting in Dr. Principal's office, I felt a little wobbly, so I decided to check in at the nurse's office. Nurse Raposo, who was the first person I'd told at school that I was a zombie, was happy to see me. She was always happy to see me. But that day, she was especially happy to see me because Sarah Anne was also there, lying down on one of the beds with her eyes closed. Ms. Frawley was sitting nearby, reading a magazine.

"Arnold, just in time!" cried Nurse Raposo. "Will you please tell Sarah Anne that being disappointed that the Yankees lost is not a legitimate reason to skip class?" I'd recently learned that in addition to horses and poetry, Sarah Anne had a very powerful obsession with the New York Yankees baseball team.

"Well, what was the score of the game?" I said, smiling.

Sarah Anne flashed her eyes at me, which was rare— she wasn't big on eye contact. Then she grabbed her letter board and started pointing.

7 TO 3, she spelled out. IT WASN'T EVEN CLOSE.

"Holy moly!" I said. "I think you should take the rest of the week off!"

"Not funny," said Nurse Raposo as Sarah Anne giggled. Ms. Frawley glanced up from her magazine and smiled.

"Why are you here, actually?" I asked Sarah Anne.

SOME MORNINGS I COME HERE TO TAKE MEDICINE,

she wrote. IT HELPS ME TO NOT GET UPSET SOMETIMES.

"Aaaah," I said.

WHY ARE YOU HERE?

I couldn't tell her the real reason—that I'd just been completely rattled by meeting one of the scientists who created me—so I just said, "I have a slight headache."

"Do you want to lie down?" asked Nurse Raposo. Ever since I'd fainted on my second day of school after taking a tiny bite of chocolate pudding, she'd kept a special eye on me. "Maybe for just a few minutes?"

I looked at Sarah Anne. "If you're ready to go to class, then I'll go with you."

She nodded and got up off the bed. Ms. Frawley put her magazine down, and the three of us headed down the hall to our classroom.

I looked at Sarah Anne, who was softly humming to herself.

If she could make it through, so could I.

A SURPRISE FROM ROSS

The first time I ever had lunch at school, I didn't know what to do, so I waited in line with all the other kids. The next thing I knew, I was holding a tray of food—pizza, a salad, something called fish sticks (I still don't really know what those are), and a small bowl of fruit.

I couldn't eat any of it, of course. So I stood there, looking lost, until Kiki called me over to her table. I didn't know it at the time, but Kiki was the kind of person who other people followed, so when she decided I was okay, everyone else kind of decided I was okay, too. Everyone, that is, except for Ross Klepsaw and Brett Dorfman. They'd had it out for me from the beginning. It didn't help matters that I was responsible for Ross getting, uh, "injured" while we played dodgeball during gym class.

Then I Zombie Zing'd Ross, and everything changed.

The Zombie Zing, just to remind you, is something only zombies can do (which is where the name comes from).

When we're threatened, we simply pinch the shoulder of the person challenging us, and they become temporarily paralyzed. The only way they can become un-paralyzed is if we pinch them again, in the same exact spot.

So what happened was, after the dodgeball disaster, Ross wanted to fight me, and he had me backed up against the locker. I basically had no choice except to Zombie Zing him.

Since no one knew I was a zombie yet, everyone just thought I was a person with some very weird abilities, and that made them very scared of me for a while. Which, in a way, was worse than people ignoring me. Because I don't want people to avoid me; I want people to like me.

Doesn't everyone?

And then a bunch of crazy things happened, like Evan's dad falling out a window and Sarah Anne running away from home, and one thing led to another, and people found out I was a zombie. Almost everyone's first reaction, of course, was fear and misunderstanding. But thanks to Kiki and Evan, and Sarah Anne, and my parents, people changed their minds and I was allowed to stay. But it was a secret. No one in the outside world could find out, or everything would be ruined.

That's why seeing Dr. Grasmere was such a shock.

I was still thinking about all of that when I went into the lunchroom, the day of the meeting in Dr. Principal's office. I had my bag of jelly beans and was just about to sit down with Evan, when I saw Ross and Brett call me over.

"Yo, Ombee the Zombie!" Ross said. "Sit with us!" They'd started calling me Ombee the Zombie after the news got out. It was pretty much the most obvious nickname in the world, but that was fine with them.

I hesitated. "You want me to sit with you guys?" Even though we were getting along okay at that point, it's not as though we were best friends. And I'd never sat with them at lunch before.

"Yeah," Brett said. "Come on, dude, we're not going to bite you."

"It's not like we're, you know, zombies or anything," Ross added, and they both cracked up. Again, not exactly the most original joke in the world, but being the subject of zombie-based comedy was becoming a part of my (after) life, and I was going to have to get used to it.

Ross put his arm around my shoulder as I sat down. "So, uh, listen, buddy, I kinda got a favor to ask."

"Sure," I said. "I enjoy doing favors. Does it have to do with tutoring for a test?"

Ross snorted. "Nah, man, of course not. I happen to be a spectacular student."

I knew for a fact that wasn't true, but I wasn't about to argue with him.

"So what's the favor?"

He looked around as if to make sure no one could hear him, even though it was incredibly loud inside the cafeteria, like always. "So, uh, yeah, I want you to train me in the ways of the zombie."

I blinked. "You what?"

Ross leaned in closer, so now even Brett could barely hear him. "I want you to train me in the ways of the zombie."

I looked around, half expecting a bunch of people to jump out from behind a wall and laugh at this hilarious joke. But no one was paying any attention to us. It appeared that Ross—who had made my life miserable for the first several months of my semi-human existence—now saw me as a role model.

All I could think to say was "Huh?"

"Dude, it's not that complicated," Brett said, butting in. "I don't get it myself, but all of a sudden everybody at school thinks you're the coolest kid around. Probably because you're some sort of science experiment, but still, you're popular, and Ross thinks if he could be more like you, then maybe he could get Kiki to like him."

Ross glared at Brett. "Dude! Are you serious right now?!?"

"Whoops," Brett said, suddenly looking like a dog who was caught ripping up his owner's favorite shoes. "I guess I wasn't supposed to say that part?"

"Uh, YEAH." Ross turned back to me. "So, I guess, yeah, there's that, too. I kind of want to maybe ask if you can find out if Kiki maybe likes me."

I glanced over to where Kiki was sitting with her friends Kendall and Shavonne. Kiki was telling a story, and her friends were listening intently. Which is usually what was happening when I glanced over at Kiki.

"I don't know," I said to Ross. "Doesn't Kiki think you're kind of a . . ."

"What?" demanded Ross. "Kind of a what?"

"I'm not sure what the right word for it is."

"Jerk?" offered Brett. "Doofus? Pizzaface?"

"We get it," Ross said to Brett, sharply. "And *you're* the doofus."

Brett shrugged, his work done. "Whatever."

I nodded. "Yeah, I guess Brett kind of summed it up. Getting her to like you would be a miracle, considering she thinks you're a jerk."

Ross threw his hands up in frustration. "That's my point! She hates me, but she doesn't really know me."

Brett scratched his head. "She's known you, like, all your life, dude. You guys went to nursery school together."

"That's not knowing someone!" Ross smacked his hand down on the table in frustration, sending a fish stick spiraling through the air. I caught it with one hand and placed it back on his tray. He took a deep breath and calmed down. "I mean, that's not *really* knowing someone. I know sometimes I come across as basically obnoxious, but I'm really not that bad." He leaned in as if to tell me a deep, dark secret. "In fact, sometimes I can actually be kind of nice."

"Well, that's good to know." I popped a jelly bean into my mouth. "I don't know if I can 'teach you the ways of the zombie,' but it may be possible to make Kiki realize you're not necessarily the irksome irritant of a person that you often appear to be."

"Okay, now that was uncalled for," protested Ross as Brett guffawed. "And also, what's *irksome?*"

"Look it up," I said. I waited for Ross to get mad and say something insulting back, but he didn't. Instead, he just nodded and said, "Okay, fine. Fair enough," and then he shook my hand. "Thanks, I really appreciate it."

Maybe miracles *do* happen.

WALKING HOME

I walked home after school with Kiki and Evan, as usual. Evan and I walked pretty slowly, since Evan had a prosthetic leg, but Kiki didn't know how to do anything slowly, so she skipped in circles around us, tapping our heads as she went by. She was talking a mile a minute about all sorts of stuff, as usual, and I laughed at all her jokes, also as usual, but Evan hadn't made a sound.

"What's up with you?" Kiki said to him, finally. "You're, like, Gary Glumface today."

He just shrugged.

"I saw you talking to Ross and Brett at lunch," he said to me. "What was that about?"

"Oh, nothing much. They had a homework question, that's all." I wasn't sure yet if I wanted to get involved with Ross's scheme, so I'd decided to stay quiet about it, for now.

Evan stopped walking. "Well, if you become friends

with those guys, then I'm not sure I can be friends with you anymore."

I stopped, too. "Who said anything about being friends with them?"

"I'm just saying," Evan said as he started walking again.

I wasn't sure what to say, so Kiki jumped in. "Arnold, you're new, so you don't really totally get it, but Ross and Brett have been making Evan miserable for years. Being friends with those guys is not really negotiable, as far as he's concerned, and I support that."

That kind of stopped the conversation in its tracks, until we headed into the parking lot by the downtown post office, which is where Evan's mom usually picked him up (she wouldn't let him walk the whole way).

"Is it possible Ross and Brett are just kind of misunderstood?" I asked. "I know they're like totally annoying and stuff, but deep down they're probably okay guys."

Evan flashed his eyes at me. "They've been calling me Crutch ever since I got cancer and lost my leg," he said, softly. "Yeah, you're right. That's not so bad, now that I think about it."

"I didn't mean it like that," I said, but then his mom drove up, honked her horn, and the conversation was over.

Kiki and I didn't talk much the rest of the way home, until we both saw a strange car in my driveway.

"Who's that?" she asked. I shrugged, pretending to have no idea. She started skipping away. "Okay, well, see you tomorrow."

She was almost out of earshot when I called, "Wait!"

Kiki turned and walked back, kicking a rock the whole way. "Yeah?"

"I . . . I just wanted to make sure you weren't mad, too."

"I'm not mad. I'm just . . . confused, I guess. I'm not sure why you would want to be nice to those guys."

"I'm not!" I said. "I mean, I'm not being nice to them. I'm just not acting to them the way they act to everyone else. I . . . I don't know how to do that."

"Okay," Kiki said. "We'll agree to disagree about that." She pointed at the car in the driveway. "Have fun with whoever that is. See you tomorrow!"

I looked at the car. I was pretty sure I knew who it was. And I was also pretty sure I wasn't going to have fun.

A SHOCK

I walked into the house, and sure enough, Dr. Grasmere was sitting there with both my parents. They all stood up when I walked in.

"Ah, there you are," said my mom, giving me a quick hug. "And how was your day?" She was talking in that kind of formal way she used to talk to me when I first came to their house, over two months ago. "Do you have any homework?"

"A little, I guess. Is it okay if I get some juice?"

"Of course," my dad said, also in a weird, distant tone of voice.

I walked into the kitchen and opened the refrigerator, where there was a pitcher of jelly bean juice that my dad had made. It was just water, crushed ice, and jelly beans, but it tasted really good, and I think it made him feel better to see me drinking something at meals. It made me look more like a normal boy.

I drank the juice down in one gulp, then went into the living room. Everyone looked at one another for a few seconds, not saying anything. Finally, Dr. Grasmere stood up. "I have a proposal that I have been discussing with Dr. and Mr. Kinder."

"You mean my parents?"

The doctor smiled slightly. "Yes, of course."

My eyes shifted back and forth between all three of them. "What kind of proposal?"

"No decisions have been made," said my mom. "We haven't said yes, and we haven't said no. We've just agreed to listen."

My dad rubbed his eyes with his hands. "What we really want, Arnold, is for you to help us make this decision," he said. "That's why we've invited Dr. Grasmere here to the house. So he can ask you himself."

Dr. Grasmere took a quick sip of water. "Thank you, Bill," he said to my father. Then he looked at my mother. "And, Jenny, you know I've always had the deepest respect for you, both as a person and as a scientist. I hope you know that."

My mom nodded without smiling. Dr. Grasmere turned his attention to me.

"I think you know most of the backstory, Arnold, and

we went over some of it this morning at school. The program was initially designed to create an afterlife species as an enemy to society. That is not common knowledge to anyone outside this immediate area. Your community has been diligent about keeping the secret, because they know that if the secret gets out, your very existence is at risk."

Personally, I felt like my existence was at risk every day, but I didn't need to mention that just then.

"As I mentioned this morning, however," continued Dr. Grasmere, "for a variety of reasons, we have concluded that it is best to modify the program considerably."

He paused, as if waiting for me to ask a question, so I did. "Modify how?"

But he didn't answer. Instead, my mother did. "Arnold, the program has taken a great deal of interest in how you've adjusted to living with humans, and your experiences as a student. As soon as they found about it, they wanted to know more."

"How did they find me?" I asked.

"We had placed a chip-inserted GPS system under the skin of every afterlife," the doctor explained. "We spent a few months narrowing down the search zone, and drone surveillance was able to pick up the signal last week."

I felt a weird buzzing under my skin, like the world was closing in around me.

"Arnold, you have to understand," my mom said to me. "There was no way this secret was going to hold forever. In this day and age, with social media and the way people gossip? Someone would have let it slip somehow. It's better for us to get in front of it." She took my hand in hers. "So, when Sherman called me, your father and I decided to fill him in—about how you were interacting so well with human society, how you were going to school, making friends—all the wonderful things that had happened to you."

My father nodded slightly. "I hope you know this wasn't easy for us, son. We wanted to tell you, but we didn't know how you'd react. Goodness knows, we couldn't have you running away again."

He was referring to the time I ran away from my friend Evan's house during his birthday sleepover, because his father—who worked for the government at the time—had realized who I was.

"So now what happens?" I asked.

My mom fiddled with her glasses, which is something she did when she felt nervous about something. "We don't have a lot of choices here, Arnold. Either we trust

Dr. Grasmere and do it his way, or they do whatever they want." Then she looked at the doctor. "Sherman, we've known each other a long time. I can only trust that you will look out for Arnold, whom I now consider my son. That you will take what he's learned, and what he's become, and use it to help all the other afterlifes."

"But you still haven't told me what the plan is," I said.

My parents and Dr. Grasmere glanced at one another, but none of them spoke.

Then Dr. Grasmere wiped his glasses with his shirt, and a sharp shiver ran down my already cold spine as I realized what he was going to say.

"I'd like to take you back to the Territory."

ANOTHER SHOCK

"**A**RE YOU SERIOUS RIGHT NOW?!?!" hollered Kiki. She looked shocked.

Evan looked even more shocked. "You're going back to, like, the lab where you were created? I thought you hated that place!"

"Yeah!" added Kiki.

It was the next day, and we were over at Evan's house, jumping on his trampoline. I was telling them about the visit from Dr. Grasmere.

"Yup," I said. "Apparently the guy was so impressed when he found out that I was going to school and had friends and stuff, that they ended up changing the idea of the whole program. Now they want to study me to figure out how to integrate all the other zombies into regular society the same way."

"Integrate?" Evan asked, and I realized I'd used a word that he didn't understand. That happened a lot, because my vocabulary was pretty advanced. I'd been programmed that way.

"What I mean is, because of me, they think maybe all the zombies can become part of society. Instead of making them the enemy, which was the original plan."

Kiki stopped jumping. "So why do you have to go back to the Territory?"

"They're going to give me a bunch of tests to see if my

brain changed somehow. And also, they want me to teach the other zombies about what it's like to live with humans."

"And your parents said you have to go?" Evan asked.

"Well, actually, my parents said it could be my decision."

"YOUR DECISION?" Kiki said, louder than she meant to. "AND YOU SAID YES?"

I took a deep breath. "I did."

"Why?" Kiki asked the obvious question.

I didn't answer, because I wasn't sure myself.

"I don't like this plan," Evan said. "What if we never see you again?"

"The doctor promised it's only for a little while," I told him, "and then I can come back home."

Evan looked like he wasn't sure he believed me. "You better."

I told Evan and Kiki exactly what Dr. Grasmere had said: that after a week at the Territory, I'd get to come back to school, where a whole team of scientists would continue to study me in my new environment. The whole goal would be to teach afterlifes the kind of behavior that would help them be accepted with actual people.

"It would really help the other zombies become part of society?" I'd asked.

Dr. Grasmere had nodded. "We have a lot of them, and at this point, it's really the only option."

And then I'd asked my mom if she agreed, and she nodded. "Trusting Dr. Grasmere is *our* only option," she said.

I thought for a second, but then realized I didn't have much to think about.

"Okay," I'd told them. "I'll do it."

After I finished telling Evan and Kiki the story, they each had the same question.

"Can we come?"

"You can do It!"

"Come on, Arnold, let's do this!"

That was my gym teacher, Coach Hank, doing his favorite thing: hollering. We were doing gymnastics, which involved a bunch of things—running, jumping, flipping—that I was not very good at. But that didn't stop Coach Hank. He wanted me to walk the whole balance beam and then jump off it, and I had no interest in doing any of that.

A girl named Cassie was trying to help me out by spotting me, but that didn't help. I kept falling off after two steps.

"How many chances is he going to get?" whined some kid in line behind me. "The rest of us want to try, too, you know."

Coach Hank glared at the complainer. "Today's his last day, so we're going to stay here all night if we have to!" He didn't mean that, of course. He would have been arrested if he'd kept us there all night.

But he was right about it being my last day. I was going back to the lab on Monday, and everyone knew about it. Everyone knew everything about me, in fact, because I was the town secret—but not for long.

I tried again and fell again. The balance beam was so long! Ross Klepsaw groaned. "I don't want to die of old age out here!"

I didn't want to die out there either, even though to be technical about it, zombies don't die ever. "Coach Hank," I pleaded, "can I stop? I appreciate the gesture, but I just don't think this is going to work."

"A couple more tries," he said. "Let's give it a couple more tries."

I tried and fell three more times. I felt a buzzing in my ears as the embarrassment started to build.

"ONE MORE TRY!" hollered Coach Hank. "MAKE IT COUNT!"

As I was climbing back onto the beam for the last time, I heard some movement behind me, near the bleachers. I turned around to see Sarah Anne taking a seat, along with her helper, Ms. Frawley. Everyone else looked over, too, because this was an unusual sight. No wait, I take that back: This was a *never-before-seen* sight. Sarah Anne didn't ever come to gym; usually she just stayed in the classroom to read, or draw horses, or write poems. But here she was, and I was pretty sure she was here to see me.

I waved. She waved back.

Then Sarah Anne asked Ms. Frawley for her letter board, and I watched her quickly spell out four words.

"YOU CAN DO IT!" yelled Ms. Frawley, announcing what Sarah Anne had written.

I smiled and climbed up on the beam. Kids started buzzing and murmuring in the anticipation of the big moment.

I started walking. Why did the beam have to be so long?

I decided to run across. Make it go faster, right? Finish with a flourish, right?

Wrong.

I made it about three steps, then felt my right foot start to slip. I tried to keep my balance but no luck.

FWOMP!

Once again—one last time—I fell facedown on the soft blue mat.

Coach Hank cleared his throat. "Uh, didn't exactly stick the landing there, Arnie." (He liked calling me Arnie, and there wasn't a darn thing I could do about it.) "Let's go ahead and call it a day, shall we?"

I nodded grimly. "We shall." I started walking out of the gym. It was so quiet you could hear a pin drop.

Finally, Ross yelled out, "Way to hang in there, Ombee the Zombie."

"Good effort, dude," Brett hollered.

"Thanks," I said to them. Then I noticed Evan and Kiki were giggling. "What's so funny?"

Kiki answered first. "You're the worst person at gymnastics I've ever seen."

"I don't think you could balance yourself on the widest sidewalk in the world," Evan added.

I was about to sarcastically thank them, when I heard the sound of one person clapping. I looked up at the bleachers, and there was Sarah Anne. She had a big smile on her face, and was giving me a one-person standing ovation.

I smiled at her and gave her the thumbs-up. She smiled back and gave me the thumbs-down.

I shook my head at her. "You, too?" Then I also started giggling, and I couldn't stop.

"Now what's so funny?" asked Evan.

It took me a minute to catch my breath. "Hard to believe that Ross and Brett are the ones trying to make me feel

better, and you guys and Sarah Anne are the ones making fun of me." I shook my head. "Boy, things have sure changed around here."

Kiki came over and threw her arms around me. "We're gonna miss you so much."

"Yeah, we are," said Evan.

I stopped laughing, suddenly remembering that I was going back to the Territory. "Well, I'll be back really soon, so you won't even have the chance to miss me."

"Are you really absolutely positively one hundred percent sure that you'll be back?" Evan asked.

"Of course I'm sure."

But the truth was, part of me was scared to death that I'd never see them again.

GOING BACK

That Sunday, the night before going back to the Territory, I was getting ready for bed (but not sleep) when my mom and dad came into my room.

"You all set?" asked my dad. "Mom said you didn't want our help."

"Yup, I'm good."

My mom sat down on my bed. "You packed the extra T-shirts I put on top of the suitcase?"

"Of course." I looked at them. "What? It's not like I'm going off to war, right? I'm going to be back in a week."

"You sure will," said my dad. "That's what Dr. Grasmere promised."

My mom took my face in her hands, which were even warmer than usual. "I want you to know that we will be in constant touch with everyone there," she said. "And we're going to be speaking every night. I know all those doctors and administrators, and they've promised to keep me up-to-date on every development. On Wednesday, your dad and I are coming to the lab to check on the progress. At that point, we'll decide whether or not it's worth it for you to keep going."

I put my toothbrush down. "Mom, why does it feel like you're having second thoughts about this whole thing?"

"I'm having second, third, and fourth thoughts, to be honest," she said with a sad smile on her face. "But once they found you—a day I knew was coming—our options became extremely limited. They were going to take you anyway. This way, at least it can be somewhat on our terms." She squeezed my shoulder. "Going back is not going to be easy, I know that. For any of us, but especially for you."

The next morning, I was on my way. The car was super quiet. At first, the only one who was talking was Lester. "Why is it like a morgue in here?" he bellowed next to me in the back seat. "Let's get some TUNES cranking!" He reached over to the radio and turned it on, and a song came on about riding a truck down a dirt road.

"Awesome!" Lester cried, before proceeding to sing along at the top of his lungs.

My parents looked at each other, but neither one said anything. They'd been doing a lot of not-saying-anything lately. They kept telling me they weren't nervous and weren't regretting the decision for me to go back, but it didn't seem that way. As a result, I was starting to get nervous, too. But here we were, in the car. It was really happening.

Lester sang:

Travelin' on that old dirt road
Carryin' a heavy ole load

Got to find what I'm lookin' for
Got to find somethin' more
This is my journey of a lifetime
So I got to find somethin' more.

Lester was the one singing his heart out, but I was the one going on the journey of a lifetime.

😵 😎 😃

The first thing I noticed was the barbed wire fence.

It appeared out of nowhere, sprouting up like some kind of evil plant along the road, mile after mile. I stared at it, and a sudden memory—well, not quite a memory, more like a fragment of a memory—flashed into my head. There were six of us, someone had me by the hand, and I was being dragged through a hole in the fence in darkness. We were escaping the Territory. I later found out that everyone else had gotten caught except me.

That was almost three months ago. It felt like a lifetime.

"We'll be there soon," my mom said from the front seat. Everyone was quiet. Even Lester.

About five minutes later, I saw the first building. It was low, almost like it was hiding from the world, but was very spread out, with tentacles sprouting in every direction. The dark brick coloring blended in with the brown ground all around it. There was very little grass, because we were in the desert. There were no flowers, and no bushes, and barely any trees. All you could see was sky, and dirt, and ground.

On the top of the building was a giant white box, which must have been the air-conditioning unit. They'd kept it incredibly cold inside the building. Most of the scientists wore jackets all the time.

Pieces of memories were coming back to me.

We pulled into a long driveway, and an armed guard was waiting by the gate. "Name, please," he said. "Who you're visiting, and cause of business."

My mom cleared her throat. "Dr. Jennifer Kinder, former director of the Afterlife Regeneration Program," she said, firmly and loudly. "I'm here to see Dr. Sherman Grasmere. We are returning Subject 48356 for a weeklong program of study and analysis."

"Subject 48356?" Lester muttered under his breath. "What the hell kind of a name is that?"

"Even worse than Norbus Clacknozzle," I muttered back.

The guard flipped through some pages on his clipboard. "Ah, yes. Please continue through the East Entrance and

report to Building Seven; Dr. Grasmere will meet you there."
Then he saluted. "And welcome back, Dr. Kinder."

"Thank you." My mom waved but didn't salute. The bar
to the gate lifted, and we drove through.

"Jeez, Ma, I'm beginning to think you were pretty
important," Lester said.

My dad smiled grimly. "You don't know the half of it,"
he said.

SAYING GOOD-BYE

Dr. Grasmere wasn't the only one waiting for us inside Building Seven. Surrounding him were a bunch of men and women who looked like doctors, plus a bunch of soldiers, administrators, and assistants.

There were also three people who looked a lot like me. They were all wearing orange jumpsuits.

Which made me realize immediately that they weren't exactly people.

Dr. Grasmere gave us a bright smile. "Welcome back to Government Territory 278—or as we like to informally call it, the Campus." His voice sounded different than it had previously. Back at the house, he was friendly and reassuring. Here he was all business. "We've got a lot to do, and not a lot of time to do it, so I'd love to get right to work." He looked at my parents. "Jenny, Bill, thank you so much for trusting us with...uh..."

"Please call me Arnold," I said. "That's my name now."

"For trusting us with Arnold," Dr. Grasmere continued. "He will be in the very best of hands and get the very best of care, that I can assure you." He turned to me. "We're all very grateful you're here. This is work that will benefit all of us, especially your fellow afterlifes."

I took a deep breath. "That's the whole idea, right?"

"It sure is." He pulled a sheet of paper out of the red folder he always seemed to be carrying. "I'd like you all to take a look at Arnold's daily schedule. It will give you some idea of how his time will be spent here."

We all crowded around the small sheet and read.

DAILY SCHEDULE—SUBJECT 48356 (REINTRODUCTION)

7 a.m.—In-Pod Breakfast

8 a.m.—Exercise Circle (morning)

9 a.m.—Civilization Training

11 a.m.—Memory Testing (Long-Term)

12 p.m.—Lunch

1 p.m.—Rest

2 p.m.—Memory Testing (Short-Term)

4 p.m.—Civilization Training

6 p.m.—Dinner

7 p.m.—Rest

8 p.m.—Exercise Circle (evening)

8:30 p.m.—Nighttime Lecture

9 p.m.—Ring of Wisdom

10 p.m.—Lights-Out

I handed the paper back to Dr. Grasmere. "What is Civilization Training?"

He glanced down at the sheet. "Ah, yes. This is one of the most important parts of the day. CT will be a series of meetings you have with some of our other subjects, in which you tell them what it was like to live in human society, and teach them some of the ways in which you learned to thrive."

"And Ring of Wisdom?" my mom asked. "That's not a term I'm familiar with."

"Yes, it's new," said the doctor. "We have realized the importance of making sure all our subjects learn the history and philosophy of this great country, now that they're going to become a part of it."

"I see," said my mom, even though judging by her tone of voice, I wasn't sure she did.

I had one last question. "When will you stop calling us subjects?"

"Oh, very soon, I'm sure." Dr. Grasmere moved toward the door, which was the cue for my parents to leave. "Well then. We will see you both in a few days, correct?"

"We'll be in touch tomorrow," said my dad.

"I'm counting on it," said Dr. Grasmere.

My parents turned to me. "Okay, kiddo," said my dad.

My mom hugged me for what seemed like about a week. Then she tapped her chest near where her heart was and said, "You'll always be right here."

"See you soon, Mom," I said. I saw a few tears roll down her cheek as she pulled back to take one last look at me. Which is when I realized something.

Zombies can't cry.

mEET THE CLACKNOzzLES

"What do you remember, Arnold? Is anything coming back to you?"

My parents had just left, and I was trying to act like everything was normal, but my insides were a jumble. Dr. Grasmere had offered me a bowl of jelly beans, but I wasn't hungry.

I nibbled on a red one. "Not really," I said. "The barbed wire outside, I guess. I think I recognized it."

"Well, that's not a surprise, since it's the last thing you saw when you sneaked out of here a while back."

Dr. Grasmere laughed, but it wasn't the kind of laugh that was friendly. It was the kind of laugh that made me a little nervous.

"Okay," I said.

He put his hand on my shoulder and squeezed. "Let's take a tour." He headed for the door, then stopped in his tracks. "Oh, hold on, where are my manners? I need to introduce you to your new roommates." The three not-quite-human-looking people in orange jumpsuits stepped up awkwardly, their eyes never leaving the floor. One was tall, and a male. One was a bit shorter than him, and a female. And there was a juvenile, about my size. She was a girl.

Dr. Grasmere said, "I want you to meet Frumpus Clacknozzle, Berstus Clacknozzle, and Azalea Clacknozzle."

I blinked a few times. They had the same last name that I had. Or used to have.

"Nice to meet you," I said to them, very quietly.

The tall male stepped forward. "I am Frumpus," he said. "Do you remember us?"

"Now, no hints, Frumpus!" said Dr. Grasmere. "You know the rules."

I closed my eyes and tried to remember. Blackness. Shouting. Running. There were blurred images in my mind, but it was like someone had placed a layer of mud over my brain.

The adult female stayed quiet, looking at the ground. I looked at the juvenile female, and she smiled slightly. And just like that, something clicked inside me.

"I know you," I said, very softly. "I know you all."

"My name is Azalea," said the young girl, stepping forward.

"You were my roommates," I said. "Until we escaped."

"We don't remember that," said the adult female. "There's a lot we don't remember."

I nodded. I myself wasn't sure which part of the story I remembered, and which part I knew only because my parents had told me about it.

The adult female, whose name must have been Berstus, looked up at me for the first time. "I will escort you to the Podhouse, where you will be staying with us," she said. "Everything is all arranged, and our domicile has been readied for your arrival."

I smiled to myself, thinking how Lester would have reacted if I used the word *domicile*. He often said that my advanced vocabulary was the most abnormal thing about me.

"I would like that, thank you," I said.

Frumpus bowed. Then Berstus and Azalea also bowed. It was all very formal. And, oddly, starting to feel very familiar as well.

Dr. Grasmere opened the door. "Let's take that tour," he said, and we headed outside into the cool desert air. He turned to me. "And to begin, Arnold, I thought I'd take you back to a place of particular interest."

"Where's that?" I asked him.

"Where you escaped." He gave me an odd smile. "Actually, not just where you escaped. *When* you escaped."

There was a sudden loud, buzzing sound. Then Dr. Grasmere shined a bright red light in my face, and everything went black.

mEMORY dREAM

"*C*ome," a voice said. "Come now. Please."

It was dark and cool. There was wind. Countless stars dot-ted the sky. I blinked, not sure who was speaking.

"There is no time. I will explain later. For now, we go."

I didn't understand what was happening. At night in the Territory, each pod returned to its tent to lie down on wooden benches. We were instructed not to speak at all. We were instructed to think about the previous day's lessons and study for the lessons of the day ahead. No one had ever spoken after curfew before. But here was Berstus, standing over me, her hand extended.

"Come."

I did what I was told. I got up, folded the blanket on my bench, and followed her out the door flap of the tent.

Already waiting outside were Frumpus, Azalea, and two other afterlifes I did not recognize.

I rubbed my eyes. Not because I was tired, but because I was having trouble believing what I was seeing.

"What is happening?" I asked.

"We're leaving," Frumpus answered. "We're leaving here forever."

I didn't understand. "I don't understand. What does 'leaving here' mean? Where else is there?"

Berstus grabbed my hand again. She was already holding Azalea's hand. Azalea looked just as confused as me. "There is much else," Berstus said. "There is a whole world else."

But she explained no further. She didn't have to. I realized what she meant.

We were going out to where the humans were.

HUMAN PROMISES

I blinked my eyes. Dr. Grasmere came slowly into focus, standing right in front of me.

"Are you back?" he asked. "Can you see me?"

I nodded.

"You just had a Memory Dream," he said, with an excited gleam in his eyes. "One of the first things we're going to study, Arnold, is how much information about the past has been stored in your brain. In addition, I am conducting exercises that will restore certain specific memories so you can remember what your previous stay here was like. It will help you reacclimate to your environment."

"But why would I have to reacclimate?" I asked. "I'm only going to be here one week."

Dr. Grasmere laughed softly and put his hand on my shoulder. "Oh yes, of course. That's true. But better safe than sorry, I say."

We stopped in front of a small yellow building, one

room really, which had a small flap on one side. "Well, here we are—this is your pod. It's getting late, and I need to get some work done. We'll begin daily activities in the morning. Your podmates will take it from here. Good night." Dr. Grasmere offered a small bow, then nodded and walked away.

I looked at the Clacknozzles, who were already inside the pod. This was where I had lived. They still lived there. I was going back to where I came from. I was going back to my old life. My old afterlife.

"Come in," said young Azalea. "I will show you your assigned space."

We went inside the pod, which was empty except for four benches, a giant jar of jelly beans, and a small basin filled with water.

"Where is the bathroom?" I asked. "I have to brush my teeth."

"Brush your teeth?" asked Berstus. "Why on earth would you want to do that?"

"Because it's—" I decided not to explain and just show them instead, so I opened my backpack and took out my toiletry bag. "This is called a toothbrush. Humans use it on their teeth to get them clean. Now I do, too."

"I did not know that teeth got dirty," Azalea said.

"Watch." I took out my toothpaste, put some on the toothbrush, and started brushing. They looked at me like I had suddenly sprouted a second head.

"You can't swallow the toothpaste because the zombie stomach can't handle it," I explained. "So you have to spit it out." And I spit into a small hole in the ground beside the basin.

"Can I try it?" asked Azalea.

I shook my head. "You will have to get your own tooth-brushes from Dr. Grasmere."

Berstus frowned and sat down on one of the benches. "Well, I must say, this activity of yours seems both pointless and disgusting," she said. "I will have no part of it."

"Humans like to be very clean," I told them. "If you are ever to live among them, you will have to be clean, too." I looked around. "So there's no shower?"

Berstus blinked. "Shower?"

Oh boy, this was not going to be easy. I helped myself to a handful of jelly beans. "You must understand, it took me several months to understand the ways of the humans. My job is to teach you what I've learned, but I'm not sure how I will be able to train you all in a week."

Frumpus frowned. "A week? Do you think you're only going to be here a week?"

I suddenly got a hollow feeling in my stomach. "Yes, of course," I said. "That is what I have been promised."

A sad look crossed Berstus's face. "You really don't remember anything, do you? If you did, you would recall the one thing they actually made sure we *did* remember."

She walked over to me and looked into my eyes.

"Humans are never to be trusted," she said. "Their promises mean nothing."

dodgEBALL AgAIN?

The next morning at eight o'clock on the dot, Dr. Grasmere burst into our pod, blowing a whistle.

"EXERCISE!"

He reminded me of Coach Hank, our gym teacher at school, who lived his entire life being incredibly loud and incredibly excited.

I'd spent the whole night, and most of breakfast, thinking about what Berstus had said. *Humans are never to be trusted.* That was what they had taught us—or more accurately, programmed into us—at the Territory. But I had met many humans whom I had come not just to trust, but to care for, deeply. My family. My friends. My teacher, Mrs. Huggle. The school nurse, Nurse Raposo. Even Coach Hank! Sure, he was kind of wacky, but I trusted him.

Did all that mean nothing?

I looked up at Dr. Grasmere. "Can I call my family today?"

"Of course!" he answered, with a bright smile. "We can even do it as a VisCall, so you can see them, too."

I felt a warm surge of relief fill my cold body. "That would be wonderful, thank you."

But before I could think about what to say to my parents, there was another blast of the whistle. "Is everyone ready?" hollered Dr. Grasmere. "Today for Exercise Circle, Arnold is going to show us all about human activities and sports."

Frumpus, Berstus, and Azalea Clacknozzle were quiet. I had noticed that whenever Dr. Grasmere was around, they never said anything at all. They just did what they were told. I closed my eyes and tried to remember if that's how I had been back when I lived at the Territory. But I couldn't recollect anything. I guess I had to wait for the next time Dr. Grasmere shined the red light into my eyes.

"What's your favorite sport?" Dr. Grasmere asked me.

"I don't have a favorite."

"Oh, come now, you must have *one*! Humans love sports!" Dr. Grasmere led us outside to a clearing in the middle of the residential area. I saw other afterlives emerging from their pods, next to staff members and other doctors. I realized they were being told to follow us.

"Are they coming?" Azalea whispered to me, with a worried look on her face.

"I think so," I whispered back. "Don't be nervous."

"I've never played a sport before." Azalea glanced up at me with a shy smile. "We practice running every day, but I'm still terrible at it."

"So is every zombie," I said.

Azalea stopped walking. "Every what?"

"Zombie." She looked at me blankly. I stopped walking. "Holy moly, that's right. You've never heard the word *zombie* before, have you?"

"No, I haven't," Azalea said. "It sounds like a very ugly word."

I nodded. "Yeah, I guess it is."

"What does *yeah* mean?"

I couldn't help but laugh a little bit. "Oh boy, do we have a long way to go."

I felt a hand on my shoulder and looked up to see Dr. Grasmere. "Your teacher told me that you're very good at dodgeball," he said. "The best in the whole school, in fact. So why don't we start with that?"

"I'm terrible at dodgeball," I told him.

"I doubt that!" He sounded one more blast on his whistle. All the afterlifes stopped walking and formed two straight lines in front of Dr. Grasmere. "Okay, everyone, listen up. Please, I need all the trainees to pay close attention. This is Arnold, and he is one of you. But he has been living out among human beings for the last several months, going to school with human children, and has done so very successfully. He is here for just one week, and he will teach us all what you need to know so you can live among the humans, too. Because that is our ultimate goal. To free you from this facility and have you live peacefully, with all the freedoms afforded to every other member of society."

I glanced at Berstus, but her eyes were fixed firmly on the ground.

"There is much to be done and learned," Dr. Grasmere

continued, "but I thought we would begin with some fun. And so, Arnold is going to teach us all how to play dodgeball, which is a very popular game among children at human schools." He tossed me a ball, which I barely managed to catch. Dr. Grasmere laughed. "Well done! Arnold, it's all yours."

Dr. Grasmere turned, walked off the field, and disappeared out of sight. The members of his staff stood with their arms folded. The other afterlifes stared at me, waiting.

I tried to imagine what Coach Hank might do in this situation.

"Okay, everyone!" I tried to holler, but it came out more like a squeak. "Circle up! Let's pick teams!"

The afterlifes shuffled toward me, dragging their legs. I was reminded of the movie that I watched with Evan and Kiki at Evan's birthday party. It was called *ZOMBIE ATTACK!*, and in the movie all the zombies moved like drunken sleepwalkers. I had considered it a terrible and inaccurate insult, until now.

"Come on, guys!" I urged. "You can do better than that!"

But, as it turns out, they couldn't.

First, I tried to introduce myself to everyone, but after a

flurry of Quickswizzles, Danktoozles, and Clupbezzles, I gave up trying to remember anyone's names.

Then I divided everyone up into two teams and had them stand on opposite sides of the field. The staff members put a bunch of red rubber balls in the middle. The afterlifes stared at the balls like they were poisonous apples.

"Okay, ready? The idea is to throw the balls at the people on the other team and try to hit them. But not in the face. And you have to stay on your side of the field.

Okay, when I say go, race in, grab a ball, and start firing. Go!"

No one moved.

"GO!" I repeated.

They continued to stare. After a few seconds, a few nervously picked up balls and held them.

"Come on, you guys!" I urged. "Game on!"

I heard one female afterlife start muttering. "What does 'you guys' mean? What a rather odd expression."

"Most peculiar indeed," agreed a male. "And what does 'game on' mean?"

I was starting to realize that the afterlifes were not all that much fun to be around.

Finally, I decided to jump-start things. I ran to the center, picked up a ball, and flung it at Azalea, who was across the field. It wasn't a hard throw—I was a zombie, after all—but it was accurate, and it plunked her square on the shoulder. She stared at me for a second, then ran off the field, moaning.

"You're out," I told her, somewhat unnecessarily.

It took a moment for everyone to absorb what I had just done. Then, as if by magic, every afterlife understood the whole point of the game: hit or be hit. In a mad dash, they all sprinted to the center. The lucky ones who managed to grab a ball quickly flung it at their unlucky opponents, who ran for their lives. Balls were flying back and forth— well, more like gently floating back and forth. Everyone was shouting—well, more like gently crying out. And those who got hit with a ball immediately started moaning, just like Azalea had.

It only took about forty-five seconds to get down to one player on each side: Frumpus and Berstus Clacknozzle.

They looked at each other from across the field.

"Berstus is my friend," said Frumpus. "I do not wish to hit her."

"It's okay. It's just a game. You can still be friends afterward."

Berstus tilted her head, as if listening to a very soft sound. "It doesn't seem like a game," she said. "Games are supposed to be fun and throwing things at each other doesn't feel fun."

"Humans are very competitive," I said. "It's the game of life—someone always has to win, and someone always has to lose."

And with that, Berstus threw the ball and hit Frumpus on his left leg.

"I win," Berstus said. "You lose."

Frumpus walked off the field moaning, just as all the others had.

Berstus walked up to me.

"Thank you," she said. "You have taught us much today."

THE ExPERImENT

After the dodgeball game, the Clacknozzles and I went back to our pod for jelly beans and water, and we were resting on our benches when there was a knock on the door. A soldier was standing there, stiffly. "Dr. Grasmere would like you all to report to his office," she said.

When we got there, Dr. Grasmere was busy reading one of his thick red folders. He didn't bother to look up. "Arnold, I hear the dodgeball game was a great success. I'd like to continue building on that momentum with our first Civilization Training session. One of the goals will be to teach your fellow afterlifes all about the various human activities at home: what they eat, what they do for enjoyment, how they groom, how they work, how they rest, how they interact with each other—the kindness, the anger . . . all the complicated range of emotions that humans show." He glanced up at me for a brief second, then went back to his folder. "If the training is successful, we will replicate it with all the other subjects on campus."

"I will try," I told him.

"Good. Follow me." Dr. Grasmere then opened a back door of his office, which led outside, to another building. "I am moving you all into a new facility that more accurately represents the living conditions of the modern human family."

He opened the door to the new building and turned on the lights. I couldn't believe my eyes. It looked exactly like the Kinders' house. *Exactly.* The wall in the living room even had the same water stain in the same spot.

"Holy smokes," I whispered.

Dr. Grasmere smiled. "I took notes," he said. "And pictures."

The other afterlifes walked around, as if in a daze. Azalea opened and closed the door to the refrigerator over and over. Frumpus flushed the toilet in the downstairs bathroom around twenty times. Berstus lay down on a bed and looked like she never wanted to get up.

"I will leave you all to it," Dr. Grasmere said. "There is a full supply of jelly beans in the cupboard. Arnold, I will see you in twenty-four hours, when your parents come for a visit."

I was shocked. "You're leaving us in here for twenty-four whole hours? What about the daily schedule?"

"Change of plan," Dr. Grasmere said as he put on his coat. "You have much to learn. All of you."

The door shut behind him with a loud *click*.

LIVINg LIKe HuMANS

Frumpus, Berstus, and Azalea lined up in front of me.

"The first thing you all have to know," I said, "is that electronic devices are the most important things in humans' lives."

I picked up the phone that sat on a charger in the kitchen. "In the old days, human beings used to talk on phones. But now they barely do that. Now they talk *through* the phones."

"We have been taught that no human being can function without one," Berstus said.

"Very good, that is correct." I put the phone down. "Later I will show you all the various functions. But since you were all so fascinated by my toothbrush, I think we'll start with grooming. I will show you how human beings wash themselves."

We all walked into the bathroom. I turned on the sink. "Human beings use water and soap. They wash their skin several times a day."

"Why?" asked Azalea.

"They do not want anything on their bodies," I told him.

"But what about makeup?" asked Berstus. "We have been taught that people put many types of foreign objects on their skin."

"Mostly women," added Frumpus.

"That is true," I said. "But then they wash it off at night."

Azalea scratched her head. "So why do they put it on in the first place?"

"They think it makes them look more appealing," I told her.

"I don't understand," said Azalea.

"Neither do I," I said, "and I've been living with them for several months."

Frumpus opened the mirror in the bathroom, which was stuffed full of creams and gels and various kinds of medicine, just like the cabinet at home. She picked up a jar of face cream, opened it, sniffed it, wrinkled her nose, and put it back.

"I have noticed that many of the female staff members here have poked holes in their ears and have placed objects in those holes," Berstus said.

"Some of the male staff members, too," added Frumpus, "but not too many."

I sat down on the couch in front of the TV, just like I did

at home. I saw a version of my dad's favorite chair, which was across the room, and immediately felt sad, until I realized I would see them the next day. "I know a girl who actually poked a hole in her nose," I told everyone. "And she has a small round piece of jewelry called a diamond in the hole." I saw the shocked expressions on their faces. "And you know what the strange thing is? It actually looks kind of nice."

I picked up a clicker and pushed a button. When the TV popped on, the three afterlifes started whispering in confusion and fear. "Sorry to startle you all," I said. "You can turn on a television with the push of a button. You can do a lot of things with a push of a button. The goal of most humans is to move as little as possible."

"Is that healthy?" asked Berstus.

"They seem to think so." I flipped through a bunch of channels. "Tonight we will watch some television. It is a very popular activity among humans. Most of them do it at night before they go to bed."

"Do they read?" asked Frumpus.

I shook my head. "Rarely."

They all stared at the TV while firing more questions at me.

"How do pictures and sounds come out of a box?"

"Is it magic?"

"Can they see us?"

A man was talking on the television. He was surrounded by falling balloons. Azalea walked up and stared into the screen. "Hello!" she said. "I am Azalea. What is your name?"

The man on the TV was shouting, "And with zero percent interest for the first year, we can guarantee the lowest prices anywhere!"

"I'm sorry," Azalea said to the man on the screen, "but are you talking to me?"

"He's not talking to you," I told her. "He's talking to anyone who happens to be watching him. He's selling something that he wants people to buy, which happens a lot on TV."

"Humans have strange habits," Frumpus said, not incorrectly.

I changed the channel, and the screen suddenly filled with a large steak, smoking on a grill. There were two women and a man standing over the grill, and the woman was saying, "So the key is to smoke the meat around the outside at a low temperature for about four hours, to tenderize it just right, and then you can season."

This time it was Frumpus who walked up to the TV. "What are you people doing?" he asked the people on the screen. "It looks very dangerous! Fire is bad! Fire can kill!"

"Okay," I said, turning off the TV. "I think we're done here."

The three afterlifes looked at me.

"What do you want to do next?" asked Frumpus.

"Take a nap," I answered, even though that was a physical impossibility.

"I would like to take a nap, too!" said Azalea. Then she thought for a second. "What's a nap?"

Indoctrination

Two hours later, I had taught my eager students several incredibly important ways to behave like a human:

- Take a lot of pictures of yourself.
- Eat until you're not hungry, and then eat just a little bit more.
- Laugh when someone makes a joke, even if it's not actually that funny.
- Never say something mean about someone else when they can hear you; wait until they're far away, then do it.

I was in the middle of showing them how to button a shirt (it's not as easy as it looks, especially if your fingers feel like they're made of jelly), when there was a knock on the door.

We all looked at one another.

"Is anybody expecting anybody?" I asked.

They all shook their heads.

"Okay, well, maybe Dr. Grasmere forgot something." I went to open the door, and there was a soldier standing there. It was the same soldier that had knocked on our tent earlier in the day, telling us that Dr. Grasmere wanted to see us. This time I noticed her name tag, which said KELLY.

"Can I help you?" I said.

She was standing at attention in her crisp green uniform. Her eyes stared straight ahead, right over the top of me. "I'm Sergeant Kelly. If you'd all come with me, I'd be much obliged."

"Again?" I asked. "We were told by Dr. Grasmere to stay here for twenty-four hours, while I started training them in all aspects of human behavior and activity."

The soldier held out her hand, which held a piece of paper. I took it.

MEMORANDUM

These orders are to bring subjects currently housed in Unit 0427-W to the South Examination Room for Memory Testing.

These orders are to be executed posthaste and without delay.

Sherman J. Grasmere
Medical Director
PROJECT Z

I handed the piece of paper back to Sergeant Kelly. "I assume this pertains to us?"

She pointed above the door. There was a small sign that I hadn't noticed before, which read 0427-W.

I turned to the others. "Okay, everyone, I guess that's enough Civilization Training for now. Time to go to our next activity."

"Will we be watching more television there?" asked Azalea.

I smiled. "Maybe, but I doubt it."

We followed the sergeant down the walkway, across a dimly lit parking lot, over a wooden footbridge, and into a brick building. The building consisted of one giant room, with white walls, a string of bright lights across the white ceiling, and absolutely no furniture. All the other zombies were already there, but there were no actual humans in the room—not even Sergeant Kelly, who had left immediately after we were inside.

The door locked with a metallic *clink*.

"We have been here before," whispered Azalea. "This is where we have indoctrination."

"Indoctrination?" I asked. "What is that? Is that the same as Memory Testing?"

But before she could answer, the same buzzing noise

I'd heard earlier filled the air. It was soft at first, but then got louder, and louder, until it got so loud I could not hear myself think. Then all the lights went out except for a single bright white light in the middle of the room, and a giant screen descended from the ceiling close to the far wall.

A man wearing a military uniform appeared on the screen.

"WELCOME," he said, in a booming voice. "MY NAME IS JONATHAN JENSEN, AND I AM THE REGIONAL COMMANDER OF THE NATIONAL MARTIAL SERVICES. I AM SO GLAD TO HAVE YOU HERE."

My head continued to buzz, even though the loud noise had stopped.

"CONGRATULATIONS. YOU ARE HERE AT THE BEGINNING. WE ARE TAKING THE AFTERLIFE PROJECT TO A NEW LEVEL."

More screens began to drop from the ceiling. The same face and the same voice began to multiply. "PREVIOUSLY YOU WERE BEING TRAINED TO THINK OF HUMANS AS THE ENEMY. HOWEVER, YOUR SYSTEMS ARE BEING RESET, AND ASPECTS OF YOUR KNOWLEDGE BASE WILL BE ERASED, THEN MODIFIED ACCORDINGLY."

We were now surrounded by screens of this giant man. There was even a screen on the ceiling. His voice echoed all around us. I looked at the others—they were staring blankly into space, as if hypnotized.

And then I realized what was happening. The indoctrination was how they took thoughts out of our heads and put new thoughts in them.

How they made us do exactly what they wanted.

"WE HAVE REALIZED THERE IS SO MUCH MORE WE CAN DO WITH YOU. IT WAS FOOLISH TO CREATE AN ENEMY WHEN THE UNITED STATES HAS SO MANY ADVERSARIES ALREADY."

The bright light began turning dark red.

"YOU WILL NOW BECOME A FORCE FOR GOOD. YOU WILL BE SOLDIERS FOR A CAUSE. YOU WILL BECOME THE

GREATEST FIGHTING FORCE THIS NATION HAS EVER KNOWN. WELCOME TO PROJECT ZW. YOU ARE NOW ZOMBIE WARRIORS."

The dark red light got brighter. After a few more seconds I had to squint.

And then I couldn't keep my eyes open at all.

FuTuRE dREAm

I am running through a field.

There is smoke and fire.

"FORWARD!" commands a voice. He is our general. "FORWARD NOW!"

There are many of us.

Afterlifes, by the hundreds.

We charge ahead.

A HERO TO THE CAUSE

YOU ARE A HERO TO THE CAUSE

YOU ARE ALL HEROES TO THE CAUSE

THE PRIDE OF OUR NATION

I clutch my rifle and my sword.

The humans are with us, yelling. "They are on the left! The left flank!"

The afterlifes are in front.

The humans are behind.

There is an explosion. Smoke billows high up into the sky. A fire breaks out.

A general is on a horse, surveying the field. He points. "I want our forces to circle around their encampment," he says, his voice calm and sure. "They will not see us coming. The element of surprise will be to our advantage."

The afterlifes stand still. We are all waiting. Waiting for our chance to shine.

The other humans surround the general. They are nodding. They have their orders.

"Listen up!" yells a captain—also a human, of course. "This is it! Men and women of Afterlife Company C, this is the moment you've been waiting for! We need your courage! We need your strength! You have nothing to be afraid of, because you cannot die! You cannot feel pain! You are the perfect soldiers! The ultimate warriors! Now you shall go and prove your loyalty to our great nation!"

The humans give out a great roar. The afterlifes nod but do not roar, because we are not capable of roaring. We are not capable of yelling, or sleeping, or breathing.

But we are capable of fighting, of defending our country, of making our human commanders proud of us.

The general blows his whistle.

We charge toward the smoke.

SCRuBBEd CLEAN

"Wake up. Wake up, son."

I stirred. No one had ever asked me to wake up before. Probably because I've never been asleep.

"Wha—what's going on?" I pried my eyes open and squinted up at Dr. Grasmere, who was wearing his usual red jacket and carrying his usual red folder. "Where am I? What happened?"

"I think you must have fainted. The sergeant here will help you up." I noticed Sergeant Kelly, standing next to Dr. Grasmere, with her hand extended. I reached out, and she grabbed me with an incredibly strong grip and pulled me up.

"Are you all right?" she asked.

"I guess so." My voice sounded scratchy and weak. I glanced around and noticed I seemed to be in a place I'd never seen before. There were couches and chairs, and a fire was roaring in the fireplace. On the wall there was a painting of a man I didn't recognize. "Where am I?" I repeated.

"Why, you're in the Visitors' Center," said Dr. Grasmere. "Your family will be here any second."

"My family?" I was confused. I had no family.

Dr. Grasmere let out a small laugh. "You have visitors, Arnold. Whether or not they're your family—well, we'll just have to see."

"Who is Arnold?" I asked. "I don't understand. I remember the dodgeball game, and showing Berstus, Frumpus, and Azalea how to watch TV and button a shirt. And then Sergeant Kelly came to get us and . . . well, I'm not sure what happened after that."

"I'll tell you what happened," said Dr. Grasmere. "You've already taught our afterlifes so much. You're doing a great job. In fact, I'm going to talk to your parents about letting us keep you for another week."

I felt a warm feeling of relief spread inside my body. "That's wonderful," I said. "I would very much like to stay. But I don't understand what you mean by 'parents.' I have no parents."

Dr. Grasmere smiled. "It would be our honor to have you."

Just then the door opened, and a large human boy burst through. "BROTHER!" the boy hollered, picking me up in a big bear hug. "I can't believe I'm saying this out loud, but I've missed you, man. A lot. Can't wait to get you back home!"

"I am not sure who you are," I said. "And I *am* home."

A confused look crossed the boy's face, like his ears had

suddenly stopped working. "Wait, what?" He poked his head out into the hall. "Mom? Dad? Arnold is saying some totally weird stuff!"

"Who is Arnold?" I asked again, but before anyone could answer, two adult humans came in, and the woman adult wrapped me up in a giant hug. "It is *so good* to see you," she whispered into my ear. She let go of me as her eyes scanned my body. "Let me look at you. Are you getting enough jelly beans to eat? All your favorite flavors?"

"Yes," I said.

The male adult hugged me next. "It's been a long couple of days, son, I'll tell you that much."

"We've been very busy," Dr. Grasmere told them.

"Really?" said the woman. She turned to me. "Have you been enjoying all the activities on the daily schedule?"

I looked at Dr. Grasmere. The truth was, I didn't know. There were gaps in my memory. "Okay," I said.

I could tell the human visitors were also confused, but before they could ask more questions, Dr. Grasmere started talking again. "There's been some wonderful interaction between Arnold and his fellow afterlifes," he told them. (I still had no idea why everyone was calling me Arnold.) "In just a short time, he's taught them so much about life in the outside world. When he returns to your family, we will be able to take what he's learned and apply it to all our subjects here, as we get ready to incorporate our community into society at large."

"When I return to my family?" I asked Dr. Grasmere. "What does that mean?"

Dr. Grasmere's tone of voice was gentle and soothing. "Well, as you'll remember, we had an agreement. After one week, you are to return to your family, and your life in school. But I'm sure we will continue to work together. You are an inspiration to all of us."

"Actually, I *don't* remember," I said. "And as I told this boy, I *am* home. This is where I belong."

The boy's eyes went wide. "See, Mom and Dad? I told you! I told you he was saying weird stuff!"

A look of panic crossed the woman's face. "Now, Arnold, we discussed this. I'm very glad you're trying to help here, but your home is with us. Your life is with us."

"This is my home," I said, yet again. I wasn't sure why they couldn't understand that. "And who is Arnold?"

"They've brainwashed him," said the man. He glared at Dr. Grasmere. "It's like you scrubbed his brain clean."

"Arnold is doing a wonderful job for us," Dr. Grasmere said.

"Stop calling me that," I said. "I am a force for good. We are all a force for good."

The woman's face turned a shade of red I'd never seen before. "Sherman, what is going on?" Her voice shook with emotion. "I need to know what is going on right now. What have you done to my little boy? I trusted you!"

"I'm very sorry you are upset, Jenny," Dr. Grasmere said, his voice soft and soothing. "But I must remind you, he is not your little boy. He is the property of the U.S. government, and as such, you are not entitled to dictate his whereabouts. Now, if he wanted to go with you, I very well might grant that request, but it appears he may want to stay here and help us a bit longer. I would hope that you would honor that desire."

The woman grabbed my hand. "Arnold, you're coming with us. You're coming with us right now."

"I don't understand," I said. The woman started to cry.

Dr. Grasmere nodded at Sergeant Kelly, who was standing at attention by the door. "Sergeant," he said, "I'm going to have to ask you to help us out for just a quick second."

Sergeant Kelly quickly stepped between my mother

and me. "Ma'am, please stand back. Please let go of the subject and stand back."

"Do not call him that," the man hissed.

"He is not a subject," the woman said, her voice sounding like steel. "He may be an afterlife, but he is also my son."

The sergeant put her hand on her hip. "I really would prefer not to have to ask you again, ma'am."

"Do you have a gun?" the boy asked. "Mom, I think she has a gun!"

"She's a soldier, of course she has a gun," said the man. He put his hand on the woman's arm. "Let go, Jen. It's okay. We'll figure this out."

The woman named Jen shook her head. "I'm not leaving without him." She put her hand on my back and started walking me toward the door.

Which is when Sergeant Kelly stepped in front of us and said, "I would advise you not to do that."

"This is my home," I said. "I am a hero to the cause."

Jen stopped. She looked at the man, and I could see a desperate look in her eyes. The man hesitated for a second, then suddenly lurched toward Sergeant Kelly. He was almost upon her when she took out some sort of weapon and fired it at the man. He fell to the floor with a grunt.

He looked up, shocked, at the sergeant. "Did you just shoot me?"

"Only with a stun gun, Bill," said Dr. Grasmere. "Next time, however, it could be different."

The woman named Jenny let go of my arm, rushed over to the man named Bill, and helped him up. "We will go," the woman said to Dr. Grasmere, with venom in her voice. "I don't know exactly what's happening here, but I will find out. And we will be back. This is not over." She walked up to me and took my face in her hands. "I want you to know something, Arnold: Zombies are people, too. No matter what they tell you, no matter what they do to you, always remember that. Zombies are people, too."

The human boy, who'd watched this whole thing frozen in place with a stunned look on his face, finally got himself to move. "We'll be back, buddy," he said. "We got this."

I nodded at the boy. Then I looked at both the adults and smiled.

"I am the pride of the nation," I said to them. "This is my home now."

A NEW NARRATOR

Evan

Hi, everyone!

My name is Evan Brantley.

I'm Arnold's best friend.

We talked it over, and we decided it would be a good idea for me to pick up the story for a little while.

And it might be fun, too!

But I should tell you right off the bat—I'm not as smart as Arnold. No one is! He's, like, the smartest kid I've ever met. And our friend Kiki totally agrees. We're both in awe of how fast he can read. It's not human! Which makes sense, since he's not human.

I don't know if Arnold told you, but back when we became best friends, I didn't know he was a zombie. No one did. That's because he and the family he was living with, the Kinders, were trying to hide it from everyone. I mean, now I get it—he had escaped from a super secret government territory where he was being programmed to attack American citizens—I think if I were him, I probably would have hidden out, too. But when I first found out he was a zombie, I was really mad. And my dad was even madder, because it was his job to make sure none of the zombies escaped from the Territory! So that got *really* complicated. But the good news is, we all decided that Arnold was awesome, and that he could stay with the Kinders, who became his parents, and Lester Kinder became his brother, and Arnold would still sit next to me at school, and the whole thing would be a secret, and no one in the whole world would have to know except for our small town.

And that worked really well for about two months, three weeks, and one day.

Until that strange man came to our school and told Arnold that he had to go back to the Territory for a week, for "further testing" and for "a new plan that was for the good of all mankind."

And Arnold agreed! And so did the Kinders!

Kiki and I thought it was crazy. Go back to the place you escaped from? Who does that?

Arnold does, I guess. Because that's exactly what he did.

Which gets us pretty much up to date.

LIFE WITHOUT ARNOLd

A day or two after Arnold left, I was eating lunch by myself, just like in the old days. Kiki had asked me if I wanted to join her table, but I said no. I guess I just felt like being alone.

I was two bites into my alfalfa sprout sandwich (my mom is kind of a health nut, and has been ever since my left leg was amputated because of cancer), when I heard a voice above me.

"Do you mind if we join you?"

I looked up and saw Ms. Frawley, the teacher's helper. Next to her was Sarah Anne, the girl who communicates by using the letter board. I had been in school with her for two years and had never really talked to her, but Arnold and she had already become friends, and so I realized that I could be friends with her, too.

"Of course I don't mind," I said. "I just happen to have a few openings at my private table."

Sarah Anne smiled at that, which made me feel good. But she wouldn't look at me. She rarely looked at anybody.

We ate quietly for a minute or two. Eventually, I said, "How is everything with you, Sarah Anne?" She nodded but kept eating.

"She wants to finish up her lunch so she can ask you something," said Ms. Frawley. I realized that Sarah Anne couldn't talk and eat lunch at the same time, because she needs her hands to do both, and I suddenly felt really embarrassed.

"Oh, gosh, I'm so sorry," I said.

Ms. Frawley smiled. "There's no need to apologize, Evan; you did nothing wrong."

"Okay." I minded my own business and waited while Sarah Anne ate. Then I noticed something else: She had a pretty impressive appetite. She ate a salad, two slices of pizza, and a bowl of chocolate pudding, and washed it all down with two milks.

I was jealous. It looked delicious.

Finally, she was done. Ms. Frawley took out the letter

board. Sarah Anne looked me in the eyes, for the first time ever, I think.

"That's her way of telling you that what she's about to say is pretty important," said Ms. Frawley.

I nodded. "Got it."

Sarah Anne turned to the board and started pointing at letters. I'd never seen her do it up close, and it was pretty amazing, how fast her hand moved. But Ms. Frawley was used to it, and knew exactly what Sarah Anne was saying. Ms. Frawley said the words out loud as Sarah Anne pointed.

"HAVE YOU HEARD FROM ARNOLD?"

I shook my head. "No, not yet. It's only been a couple of days, and I don't think he's allowed to have a phone in there or anything. Why, have you?"

Sarah Anne shook her head, and started writing again. "I AM WORRIED."

"Worried? Why?"

"I DON'T KNOW I JUST HAVE A BAD FEELING."

"You mean about him going back to that place?"

Sarah Anne nodded.

"What's going on over here?" asked a voice behind me that I recognized. It belonged to Kiki, my other

best friend besides Arnold. Kiki had a very recogniz-able voice. Kiki had a very recognizable everything. She was probably the most popular kid in our whole grade, but for some reason, she had decided that she wanted to be friends with me way back in kindergarten and has stayed friends with me ever since. Who was I to argue?

Kiki plopped down on the seat next to me. "What are you guys talking about?"

"Arnold," I said.

"What about him?"

"Sarah Anne has a bad feeling about him going back to the lab."

Kiki turned to Sarah Anne. "I was thinking the same thing! And that doctor guy who was snooping around the school the other day seemed kind of creepy . . . the way he smiled was just . . . I don't know. I didn't trust him."

"HE REMINDED ME OF MY DENTIST," said Ms. Frawley, on behalf of Sarah Anne.

Kiki let out her loud laugh. "HA! That's never good."

Sarah Anne's fingers flew across the board. "WHAT SHOULD WE DO?"

When there was a decision to be made, or a question that needed an answer, I usually waited for Kiki to speak. She was great at making decisions and answering questions. But this time, she looked at me. "Evan, what do you think?"

I thought for a second. I hadn't really worried much about what had happened with Arnold. He seemed to want to go back to where he came from, and his parents had agreed. And it was just for a week. But now I was starting to wonder.

"I think we should investigate," I said.

"INVESTIGATE HOW?" asked Sarah Anne.

"I'm not sure," I said. "But I know where to start."

A FRIENd IN TROUBLE

Bernard J. Frumpstein Elementary School was part of a big complex where all the schools in our town were located: That was a bad thing if you didn't want bigger kids to do things like knock your cap off your head, but it was a good thing when you needed to find an older kid after school.

And there was a particular older kid we were looking for that day.

Sarah Anne went home right after school—she always did, Ms. Frawley told us—but Kiki and I waited at the bus circle until we saw Lester Kinder coming out of the high school. You couldn't miss Lester, with his big head of hair, his open backpack spilling papers out onto the sidewalk, and his loud laugh echoing off the walls of the concrete buildings. He was walking with a girl who had pink hair on one side of her head, and green hair on the other.

"That's Darlene," Kiki said. "She's, like, the coolest kid in school. Why she's friends with a big goofball like Lester is one of the world's great mysteries."

Like why you're friends with me, I thought to myself but didn't say out loud. What I did say out loud was, "Sometimes different kinds of people make the best friends."

Kiki raised her eyebrows. "What are you, a fortune cookie?"

I ignored her and walked up to Lester. "Excuse me, Lester? Do you have a second?"

"Oh, hey, Evan. Hey, Kiki. What's up?" He gestured toward his multicolored-haired friend. "This is, uh . . . my, uh . . ."

"I'm Darlene," she said.

"Hey," we all mumbled.

"So Evan wanted to ask you something," Kiki said. "About Arnold."

Lester's face darkened. "Arnold? You know what's going on with Arnold?"

"I love Arnold," said Darlene. "He's a spectacular little dude."

Kiki and I both shook our heads. "Actually, we don't

know anything," Kiki said. "We were just a little worried, is all."

Lester and Darlene glanced at each other, and I felt a knot in my stomach. "Why, is something wrong?"

Lester looked back down at us and whispered, "Come with me. Quick."

He took off running and went around the side of the high school building. The rest of us followed. He didn't stop until we were way out of sight of the people starting to line up for the school buses. I was last to get there, obviously. We were all a little out of breath.

"Sorry to make you run, little man," Lester said. "I know it's not easy, with your leg and all."

I shook my head. "It's fine. What's going on with Arnold?"

Lester looked both ways, even though there wasn't another person in sight. "It's not good. I was just telling Darlene that I don't think Arnold's coming home for a while. If ever."

The pit in my stomach turned into a full-blown canyon. "What do you mean?"

"We went to visit him yesterday," Lester explained. "First of all, he acted like he didn't know who we were.

And second of all, he was saying the weirdest stuff, like he was a warrior hero, and he was doing what he was always meant to do. It was like he was brainwashed—like, reprogrammed or something. And my parents got really upset, of course, and so they said they were taking Arnold home, but the guy, Dr. Grasmere, he said it was Arnold's choice, and Arnold said he wanted to stay, and then my mom grabbed Arnold, and we were about to leave, but there was this lady soldier there, and she had a gun, and she got in the way of my parents when they tried to take Arnold. So we left him there, and now my parents are trying to figure out what to do."

Lester took a deep breath, like he was worn out from telling us that story. Darlene squeezed his hand. "This is really weird," she said.

"Sarah Anne was right," I said, suddenly feeling mad at myself for not also being worried about Arnold.

"It's not your fault," Kiki said, as if she were reading my mind. "It's nobody's fault except that horrible doctor guy who was obviously lying to all of us. I guess the question is, what's he up to? What does he want with Arnold? And doesn't he know we can just go tell people whenever we want to and the secret will be out?"

"Maybe he's after us, too," I whispered. "Maybe he's after the whole town."

Lester shook his head. "Yo, let's not get crazy, little man. I think maybe you've watched too many scary movies."

"I love scary movies," Darlene said. "But I don't like scary real life. Scary real life stinks."

Lester picked up his backpack and threw it over his shoulders. "Hey, if you guys want to, you can come back to our house with us. My parents are home right now trying to figure out what their next move should be. They can give you more information. But yeah, you're right— looks like our little zombie buddy's in trouble."

Kiki looked at me. "Should we go?" she asked. "I can call my mom and tell her to pick us up there."

I nodded. "Yeah, I do want to go. And I know someone else who can help us, too. He's the perfect person to call in this situation."

"Oh yeah?" Lester said. "Who's that?"

I tried not to look too proud of myself. "My dad."

MAKING A PLAN

I should pause here for a second to remind you guys—in case you don't remember—who exactly my dad is. For years, Colonel Horace Brantley was the regional commander of the National Martial Services. Meaning, he was in charge of making sure our whole part of the country was kept safe, and no one did anything to threaten our security. Part of his job was to protect the Territory, and the scientific experiment known as Project Z. And part of his job protecting Project Z was to make sure all the zombies were present and accounted for. When Arnold and the five other zombies escaped, it was my dad's responsibility to catch them. And he caught them all, except for Arnold.

Now here I was, asking him to help us figure out a way to get Arnold out of there again.

Boy, times had sure changed.

By the time we got to Lester's house, my dad was

already there, sitting in the kitchen with Mr. and Mrs. Kinder. They all had very concerned looks on their faces.

"Oh, hey, kids," my dad said. "Jenny and Bill were just filling me in. This is a tricky situation, there's no doubt about it."

I got right to the point. "What are we going to do?"

"I'll tell you what we're going to do," Mrs. Kinder said. "We're going to have Colonel Brantley talk to his old friends at the Martial Services, and we're going to get local and state police on the case, and then we're marching right over to the Territory and getting our son back."

"Not so fast," Mr. Kinder said to his wife gently.

My dad cleared his throat. "Let's just think about this for a second, everyone. We don't want to do anything too hasty here, or too illegal. I would recommend a calmer, more measured course of action. We'll find you a good lawyer, file a motion in court, and begin legal proceedings as soon as possible."

Mrs. Kinder shook her head violently. "That could take weeks, maybe months, and we don't have that kind of time! Arnold has already been brainwashed to the point where he doesn't even remember who we are!"

"Easy, honey," said Mr. Kinder, rubbing his wife's back.

"I know I'm asking you to show a little patience," said my dad. "But the most important thing is getting Arnold back. And we need to go about it the right way."

"I don't get it," I blurted out. "Once we get Arnold out, won't they come after him again? Won't they, like, send the whole army this time, and not just some lousy lying doctor?"

My dad couldn't help but smile. "That's a reasonable question, Ev. But here's how I see it. Once we get this thing into the courts and out to the public, who do you think people would support: the big bad government conducting experiments in secret, or a young innocent zombie just trying to go home to his loving family?"

"I like the way you think," said Mr. Kinder to my dad.

My dad stood up and looked at me and Kiki. "If I'm not mistaken, you two have some homework to get to. Why don't you guys go out to the car? I'll be there in a second."

"Okay, Dad." We said our good-byes to the Kinders, and to Lester and Darlene, and headed outside. I was quiet, just thinking about all the things we had heard that day.

Kiki, meanwhile, was her usual jumpy, hyper self. "You

know why your dad sent us out here first, don't you?" she asked me. "You know what they're talking about, right?"

I shrugged. "Not really. I mean, I guess they're talking about the plan, like how to get a lawyer and stuff, right?"

"Yup." Kiki started kicking one of the tires of the car. "Your dad is in there telling Arnold's mom and dad how patient they have to be and how important it is to do things the right way."

I could tell by the way she said it that she was up to something. I watched her kick harder and faster. "It makes sense, though," I said. "They're adults. We're kids. They should decide what to do, obviously."

"No, it doesn't. It doesn't make sense at all." She stopped kicking and stared at me intently with her laser-like eyes. "Because what if they're wrong? What if actually, we have a better idea?"

"Uh, what kind of idea?"

Kiki looked right at me, her eyes shining. "Like, we go to the Territory ourselves and rescue Arnold."

I wasn't sure I'd heard her correctly. "You mean, like break him out? Help him escape?"

"That's exactly what I mean. We're going to help him get out of there, with or without the adults."

I felt a small bead of sweat pop out on my forehead. "Uh . . . we are?"

"Yup, we sure are." Kiki smacked me on the shoulder, which actually hurt a little, not that I would ever admit it, and then she flashed her famous grin. "And we're gonna get Lester and Darlene to help, and we're gonna be heroes, and that's all there is to it."

THE STREN9TH

Arnold

The day after the visit from the people who said they were my family, there was a knock on our pod door. There was a human standing there—Commander Jensen, the man from the videos.

"NORBUS CLACKNOZZLE!" he barked, so loud that I jumped.

"Yes, sir?"

Commander Jensen didn't look at me. "Nothing. I just wanted to say your name out loud. You have your given name back now, and you should be very proud of it."

"I am very proud of it, sir."

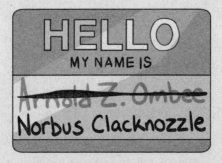

He gave out a satisfied grunt. "Terrific. Now get in formation, Clacknozzle, before I make you run extra sprints and eat chocolate cake."

I winced. The sprints wouldn't have been so bad, but the chocolate cake might have put me in the Infirmary for a week.

We all followed Commander Jensen outside. "COMPANY, FALL IN!" he hollered, into some sort of loud machine he was holding. "It is time for weapons distribution!"

Every zombie in the Territory—if I had to guess, I'd say about three hundred—gathered outside on the Ring of Wisdom in front of the pods, which was where we'd played dodgeball on my first night back.

"What weapons?" I asked Azalea, who was standing right next to me.

"I have no idea," she said.

When we were all lined up, the commander walked up to a giant truck and opened the back. Inside were a bunch of boxes that all said THE INFIRMARY on them.

"Pods C, D, and E, please remove the boxes from the truck and place them by the flagpole," he ordered.

I was in Pod D, so I ran up to the truck, grabbed a box, and put it where I was told.

As soon as all the boxes were in place, Commander

Jensen instructed each brigade to go up to the boxes one at a time and take their weapons. When it was my turn, I reached down into the box and pulled out a small container. I opened the container and it contained a single green pill.

What on earth is this? I said to myself.

I looked around, and it looked like every afterlife was wondering the same thing.

"I know what you're thinking," said the commander. "You want to know what you have in your hands and how it can help you in battle. That is a good question, and a fair question. And the only way I can answer it is this: Please swallow the pill."

Nobody moved.

"Do not be afraid!" The commander held up a small container of his own. "This weapon is called The Strength. Our scientists have been developing it for years, and we are finally ready to try it out in experimental form. And how fortunate that you have been chosen to try The Strength first! If all goes well, this weapon will help our nation become the greatest fighting force the world has ever known." And with that, Commander Jensen held up the container. "You will now swallow The Strength."

We all did as ordered, then looked at one another and waited a few seconds. Nothing seemed different.

"Take a single step forward!" ordered the commander.

I did as I was told, and found myself two hundred yards across the field from where I'd just been standing.

"Holy smokes," I said.

"Jump!" ordered the commander.

I jumped and found myself on the roof of a building. I looked around and saw zombies on top of buildings all over campus.

"Jump down!"

We jumped down and landed back on the ground.

Commander Jensen smiled. "So now you see," he said. "You see what we have been working toward all this time."

He paused, and I was about to start clapping, when I saw three zombies sway back and forth, then suddenly start to run as fast as they could—backward. Then *all* the zombies starting running backward—including me. We yelled in alarm and confusion.

"What is happening?" someone wailed as they whizzed by me in reverse.

Dr. Grasmere suddenly appeared next to the commander. I heard his voice—"EVERYONE, PLEASE STAY CALM. I CAN ASSURE YOU, NO ONE IS IN DANGER."

The only problem was, right when he said *danger*, we all began to flap our arms wildly while shouting the alphabet backward. Then, as one, every zombie fell to the ground and started flopping like fish. Green zombie sweat started pouring out of our shoes as we waited for the effects of this "weapon" to wear off.

"THERE ARE OBVIOUSLY STILL A FEW KINKS TO WORK OUT IN THIS EXPERIMENTAL PROGRAM," yelled Dr. Grasmere, struggling to be heard above our alarmed cries. "BUT REST ASSURED, WE WILL ADDRESS THESE CONCERNS, AND BE READY TO GO IN A FEW SHORT WEEKS."

As I lay on the ground, thrashing about with all the other zombies, one thought crossed my mind.

Ready to go where?

HOW TO EAT LUNCH LIKE A HUMAN CHILD

Later that day, after we'd all recovered from The Strength—or, more accurately The Strength, Followed by the Thrashing—Dr. Grasmere pulled me aside and asked me to pay special attention to Azalea, and give her individual instruction. "She is our only other juvenile on campus, besides you," he said. "As we get ready for our immersion into society, it's important for Azalea to understand what life would be like during a typical school day."

He took us to a room that had been set up to look like an elementary school cafeteria—*my* elementary school cafeteria, in fact. It looked exactly like it, right down to the missing ceiling panel next to the table where you returned your trays.

"Holy smokes again," I said.

Dr. Grasmere half smiled. "I told you I took notes."

"You weren't kidding."

He bowed. "I shall leave you two to it," he said, and left.

I went into the kitchen area, and Azalea followed. "Now, here is where human children collect their lunch," I told her. "They get a lot of food on their trays, and it is many different colors, but they seem to like the yellow and brown food the most and the green food the least."

"Why?"

"I have no idea. And there is no blue food. Ever."

"I don't understand," Azalea said. "Why do you remember some things about your life outside but not other things?"

"What do you mean?"

"I mean, you remember what lunch was like in school, but you said you didn't remember the people who said they were your parents."

I thought about that for a second but had no answer. "I don't know," I said.

"I think it is because of how they teach us to think," Azalea said. "And what they want us to know."

I nodded. "Perhaps. But whatever they are teaching us, and whatever they want us to know, it is for our own good, and the good of the nation."

Azalea didn't respond to that. Instead, she said, "Did you like life out there? Did you feel . . . free?"

"I . . . I don't know," I said. "It's like I remember

everything but the actual people." The truth was, every time I felt a memory of a person starting to form, I heard the buzzing in my head, and I saw the red light in my eyes, and my brain started to hurt.

I shut my eyes tightly and tried to remember. "There was . . . a boy and a girl. Humans. I think . . . they were my friends." But then my head started to ache so badly I had to stop.

"Are you okay?" Azalea asked, but I didn't answer. She

touched my arm lightly. "I'm sorry if that was hard," she said. "I think . . . I think someday I would like to be free like you were. If only for a little while. And even if the memories fade."

I waited a few more seconds for my head to clear, then walked with Azalea into the main dining area. She was right—for some reason, certain memories were as clear as day. "The children sit at these tables, in groups," I told Azalea. "They tend to group together in formations based on friendships and gender. And there is a certain structure in place, where the most popular kids sit with each other, leaving everyone else to find a place where they belong."

"That sounds difficult," Azalea said. "Do some children not find a place to belong at all?"

"Yes," I said, and I had a memory flash, of a boy eating lunch by himself. He was familiar, and then he was gone.

"That sounds sad," Azalea said. "Why don't they just assign the children places to eat so that the children don't have to worry about it?"

"I don't know. It's a good question, and I will bring it up when I go home."

Azalea gave me a funny look. "But you're not going back to school, remember? You're staying here, with us. You *are* home. You've said so yourself many times."

"Oh yes, that's right, of course I am!" I pretended to laugh it off, but the truth was, I wasn't sure what was happening. My mind felt jumbled. I knew I was home, I knew I was where I was supposed to be—but sometimes, something would trigger a memory, and images flashed into my head, like a bed, or a classroom, or a boy eating lunch alone, and I could see a different world entirely—if only for a moment.

It was confusing and scary, but I didn't want to say anything to Dr. Grasmere. Because if I did, he would have shined another red light in my eyes until I went into another Memory Dream.

And for some reason, I knew I didn't want that.

SPIES

Azalea and I were just wrapping up our "How to Act like a Kid at Lunch" lesson when I saw two afterlifes go into a small private room next to the cafeteria and sit down.

I didn't know their names, but I knew who they were. I'd noticed that they always stuck together, and even for zombies—who can't yell—they were very quiet. I'd almost never heard them speak, and when they did, it was only with each other. But when they came in that day, I realized two things right away. The first was that they didn't notice Azalea and me. The second was that they were joking, laughing, and talking loudly.

"Gosh," Azalea said, "what do you think is up with those two?"

"I have no idea, but be quiet." For some reason, I decided it was a good idea for them to not know we were there.

I kept watching as one of the afterlifes opened a bag he'd

brought with them into the cafeteria and pulled something out. I could smell it right away—human food.

"This is very strange," I whispered. "If they eat that, they'll be so sick they won't be able to move for weeks."

"Maybe they're just practicing what it would be like to eat lunch with a bunch of humans, like we did," suggested Azalea.

"Yes, that could be it," I said.

Azalea stood up. "Should we join them? We could practice being a family!"

I quickly pulled her back down. "No. I mean, not yet. I think they probably want to be alone."

There was something in the tone of my voice that made Azalea stop talking. I stopped talking, too. We both just watched as the two zombies each unwrapped a cheeseburger. Then one of them pulled something else out of the bag—two bottles of soda. The cheeseburgers and the drinks lay undisturbed on the table as they discussed something quietly, and with great intensity.

"Wow, they're really making it look real," whispered Azalea.

"Shhhh," I said. "Let's not disturb them—they're deep into their research." They were deep into something, I knew that much, and I needed to keep an eye on them.

Sure enough, about two minutes later, one zombie stopped talking and reached for one of the cheeseburgers. He looked at it, unwrapped it, and then did something bizarre, disturbing, amazing, and shocking.

He took a bite.

"Oh no!" Azalea said, trying to whisper and barely succeeding. "Doesn't he know what is going to happen to him?"

"I guess not," I whispered back. "Let's see what the other one does."

The second zombie watched the first zombie dig into his cheeseburger, then said something, and they both laughed. The second zombie then unwrapped his cheeseburger and took a big bite of his own. They both took generous swigs of their sodas.

"I knew it," I told Azalea. "As soon as they sat down, I had a feeling they were up to no good. They are obviously outsiders trying to sabotage our entire project. I need to alert Dr. Grasmere right away."

But as soon as I got up, Dr. Grasmere himself entered the cafeteria. "Oh, good," I said. "He'll catch them red-handed. Everything will be okay."

But he didn't catch them red-handed. Or blue-handed, or purple-handed, or any other color handed. Instead, he sat down and said something that made them both nod.

Then they offered him a cheeseburger of his own, and he took a big bite.

Okay, now *that* I didn't expect.

I stood up.

"Norbus, what are you going to do?" asked Azalea, with alarm in her voice. But I didn't answer, because I didn't know. Instead, I marched over to their table. When I was just a few feet away, they looked up and saw me coming.

The two cheeseburger-eating zombies looked undisturbed, but Dr. Grasmere had a shocked look on his face. "Norbus... Norbus, I didn't realize you would still be in here... This isn't what it looks like... I can explain everything..."

"I CAN EXPLAIN EVERYTHING AS WELL," I said in the loudest voice I could muster. "I am proud to be an afterlife, and I'm ready to fight for my country. But now I realize you have not been honest with me, and I am concerned. I am very concerned."

Dr. Grasmere wiped his face. "I understand your concern, Norbus, and I completely understand. And I apologize for misleading you. You, of all the afterlives here, deserve to know the truth." He gestured toward the two others. "And the truth is, these are not afterlifes at all. They are human men—brothers, Jim and Rick Bellweather, who are soldiers in the National Martial Services, and have embedded with the zombie warriors so that when the time comes, they can be the liaisons between the two forces as we engage with the enemy."

"Sorry about the misunderstanding," one said, sticking out his hand. "I'm Rick. No hard feelings?"

I shook his hand as the other one nodded. "I'm Jim. Thanks for the dodgeball game—that was fun. Let's do it again sometime."

I shook his hand, too, then turned back to Dr. Grasmere. "I'm not sure I understand," I said. "You have told us that we are going to be immersed with human society, but you have also told us that we are training to help defend the country against aggressive invaders. Which is it? Are we being attacked? Is a battle imminent?"

Jim and Rick got up from the table. "We better get back to it," they said. "Nice meeting you, Norbus."

By this time, Azalea was at my side. "What's going on?" She asked me. "Who were those guys?"

Before I could answer her, Dr. Grasmere gently put his hand on her shoulder and guided her out the door of the cafeteria. "It would be great if you could just give us two minutes alone," he told her. "Norbus will meet you back at your pod."

Once she was gone, Dr. Grasmere came over to where I was standing. "Have a seat, Norbus."

I did as I was told.

"You asked if you're going to be immersed into society or used as a fighting force to attack an enemy," Dr. Grasmere said. "The short answer is . . . both."

"I'm not sure I know what that means," I said.

He sat in the chair next to me, with the half-eaten cheeseburgers between us. The powerful smell of grease and meat made me a little woozy. Dr. Grasmere saw my face and quickly scooped up the human food, then got up and threw it in the trash.

"Having you back on campus has been so terrific," he said. "You've given us invaluable contributions on what life is like as an afterlife living in human conditions. It's worked out better than I could have imagined."

"I'm pleased," I said, not sure where this was going.

"So, Norbus, I'm going to tell you something very confidential, because you deserve to know it. You've already done so much for the cause."

"I have?"

"You have." Dr. Grasmere leaned in closer to me, to the point where I could smell the coffee on his breath—also not an aroma I particularly enjoyed. "You know that we are no longer planning to use the afterlifes as a military force to attack our citizens, correct? Rather, we are training you to be soldiers on behalf of our great nation."

"I do know that."

He lowered his voice, even though no one else was in the room. "Terrific. And toward that end, we are also planning to incorporate some of you, such as yourself, back into regular society, in sort of a watchdog capacity."

"Watchdog capacity? What does that mean, exactly?"

"Well, it's pretty simple, really. The afterlifes will be working with local, state, and federal governments and law enforcement agencies to monitor various activities of the communities and families within which they live and serve."

I thought for a second. "You mean, like spies?" I had a sudden memory flash of a school lunch table, and telling human children that I was a spy, and them believing me and asking many questions about it. But I couldn't see any of the human children clearly.

Dr. Grasmere laughed, but not because anything was funny. "Oh, no, no! We would never suggest such a thing. It's more like just making sure everyone and everything is functioning smoothly in such a way that is best for a peaceful and prosperous society."

"Would I tell them what I'm doing?" I asked.

"Well, to be honest, probably not. That's not quite how this program would work. You see, there is some resistance building against the government, which is the reason we are implementing this program." Dr. Grasmere paused. "And to be quite frank, there are some specific targets whom you can help us keep an eye on." He paused. "Those people who claimed to be your parents, for example. We're starting to consider the possibility that they can't be trusted. That's where you come in."

Those people who claimed to be your parents.

I thought of their faces, when they came to see me. The warm arms of the woman, hugging me. The strong arms of the man when he shook my hand. Did I know them?? Maybe I did.

"Are you saying that those people who said they are my parents are dangerous? That they're enemies?"

Dr. Grasmere shook his head. "Not necessarily. They are probably very good people. The woman is a fine scientist. But they have been known to have certain associations with certain groups that we do not believe have the nation's best interests at heart."

"What kind of groups?"

"Well, that's what we need you to find out."

I continued to open and shut my eyes, careful not to look at the lights above.

"When will I be returning to the outside world?"

"That has yet to be determined," said the doctor. "There is one last important training exercise that we must complete before we send you back out into the field."

"What kind of exercise?"

"You will find out tonight. It is an exercise that all warriors must go through to prove they are ready for the ultimate challenge in any battle."

"And what is that?"

"You are an inquisitive one, aren't you," Dr. Grasmere said, smiling slightly. "The ultimate challenge in any battle is to overcome and defeat any enemy." He got up from the table and walked to the door of the cafeteria. But before he left, he turned back to me. A small, sad smile crossed his face.

"Even if the enemies are those we love."

He left and closed the door. Suddenly I felt the buzzing in my head again. The lights above me turned a dark red. Or was I imagining it? I was confused. There was much I didn't understand, and much I didn't trust.

You can become someone we are all proud of.

Serve your country and you save yourself.

We will help you.

I shut my eyes.

I held my hands over my ears.

I felt a small part of myself start to resist.

OUTSIdE—THURSdAY, 6:57 P.m.

Evan

"Evan!" my mom screamed up the stairs. "Dinner!"

I was halfway down the stairs, when I heard another shriek. "And wear a sweater! It's chilly down here!"

I loved my mom, but she treated me like I was a ninety-two-year-old man. I think it's because I had cancer as a little kid: She was so freaked out about the possibility of losing me that she's smothered me with a blanket of overprotection ever since. And the idea of arguing about it with her? Forget it. I turned around and got a sweater.

"What are we having?" I asked when I sat down at the kitchen table.

"Spaghetti and meatballs, your favorite!" She was half-right. It would have been my favorite if it were actual spaghetti and meatballs, instead of gluten-free spaghetti and vegan tofu-balls.

As I sat down and tried to pretend to enjoy the food, my phone buzzed. A text from Kiki: **Guess who I'm with?**

"No phones at the table," my mom said, without looking up. She never had to look up to tell that I was on the phone. Moms just know.

"I forgot to wash my hands," I said, getting up from the table. My mom looked at me and raised her eyebrows, but she didn't stop me. She liked it when I got texts. That meant someone cared enough to reach out to me and send me a message. That didn't happen very often, except with Kiki. Kiki reached out a lot.

I texted her back: **I give up, who?**

I waited for two seconds, and then a picture came back: Kiki and Sarah Anne, sitting on Kiki's back porch, drinking lemonade.

No way! I texted.

Way! she texted back.

There were very, very rare occasions where an actual phone conversation was called for, and this was one of those times. I swiped her name on speed dial.

"Sarah Anne is at your house?"

I could almost hear Kiki roll her eyes. "No, it's just a

girl that looks exactly like her. Of course she's at my house!"

"Why? What? How?"

"Today in school she asked me if we'd heard from Arnold, and I told her no, but that you and I had decided we were going to rescue him."

I paused. Half of me was incredibly excited that this might actually be a possibility, half of me was incredibly nervous at the idea of trying to pull off something crazy like that, and half of me was incredibly irritated at the idea that Kiki and Sarah Anne were meeting about it, and I wasn't invited.

I know that means I have three halves, but I couldn't help it—that's how I felt.

"So wait," I said, trying to sound like a completely normal person with only two halves. "You're planning this without me?"

"Don't be silly!" Kiki giggled. "I was just telling her about the plan to make a plan." She paused. "Hold on . . . Sarah Anne is saying something . . . she says, 'Why don't you come over and we can figure it out together?'"

"Wow, uh, cool, tell Sarah Anne maybe . . ." Two more halves just popped up: pleasure at being asked, and fear about the answer to the question I was about to ask. "So, I guess you guys are thinking that we would do this without telling our parents, right?"

Kiki didn't answer for a few seconds, but I could hear her breathing. "There's no way your mom would ever let you do something like this," she finally said, stating the obvious. "And I'm pretty sure my parents wouldn't either. What about you, Sarah Anne? . . . Yeah, she says no way."

"Great," I said. "So what are we supposed to do, hitchhike there? Or maybe hop on the back of a freight train, like they used to do in those old movies my parents like to watch?"

"I think we bark up the same tree we barked up last time," Kiki said.

"What the heck does that mean?"

Kiki giggled again. "I'll give you a hint: The tree has a girlfriend with multicolored hair and an earring in her nose."

INSIdE—THURSdAY, 8:14 P.M.

Arnold

We were all gathered at the Ring of Wisdom, in a big circle. A big light hung down over the center of the Ring. Rick and Jim Bellweather stood underneath it.

"GOOD EVENING, AFTERLIFES," shouted Rick. "We can now tell you who we really are. We are humans. We have embedded with the afterlife community to learn how best to train you as Zombie Warriors. You have proven to us through many weeks of training that you will soon be ready to venture out into the world and help us defend our nation's interests."

The red light went on, and everyone cheered. I tried not to look at it.

Rick stepped back, and Jim stepped forward.

"Tonight, we begin our Ultimate Test," Jim said. "Sometimes, in battle, we learn that things aren't always as they seem. We discover that we can't be sure who are our friends and who are our enemies. And sometimes, we have to make very difficult choices. Tonight, we learn how to make those difficult choices." He paused and walked around the circle, making eye contact with each afterlife. "Dr. Grasmere will ask two of you to step into the ring to start us off. Please pay attention to see if your name is called."

Everyone in the circle looked around, eyeing each other, wondering who would be picked. I was pretty sure I knew, though.

Dr. Grasmere stepped into the ring, took out a piece of paper from his jacket pocket, and unfolded it very slowly. He looked it over for a few seconds, then looked up.

"Norbus Clacknozzle, would you enter the ring, please?"

All heads turned in my direction. I entered the ring, excited but confused. I wanted to prove myself, but I was starting to doubt what I was proving myself *for*.

"Azalea Clacknozzle, would you enter the ring, please?"

That surprised me. Dr. Grasmere had decided to have the two youngest subjects face off first. Azalea blinked twice, then walked to the middle of the circle next to me.

"In battle, we make difficult choices all the time," said Dr. Grasmere. "We face difficult decisions. And sometimes the hardest decision of all is to figure out whom you can really trust. Is the person you thought was your friend, truly your friend? What if they're actually your enemy, plotting against you? Do you have the strength, courage, and will to put aside your feelings for that person, and do what you have to do to defeat them? That is the true test, and the true definition of a warrior."

Azalea turned to face me. I couldn't see her eyes, and I wondered if she could see mine. Twilight was approaching, and shadows were beginning to fall. We waited for further instructions.

Dr. Grasmere swept his hands dramatically toward my opponent. "Azalea is not one of us."

A tremor of shock went through the crowd. I couldn't believe my ears.

"She is indeed an afterlife," said Dr. Grasmere, "but she is an afterlife who was sent here by an alien nation who wants to destroy us. She has studied our ways so she can report back on how to defeat us."

"That is not true," Azalea said, with panic in her voice. "None of it. None of it is true."

"I don't understand," I said. "When I first got back here, you told me she was one of the zombies that escaped with me. We have trained together the whole time." I glanced at Azalea, then glanced away. "We have become close."

Dr. Grasmere raised his voice. "We have all worked too hard and held on to this dream for too long to have it jeopardized by an Outsider—an interloper. Norbus, we call on YOU to punish this afterlife and to withdraw her power to function." He held up his hand, and there was utter silence. "We call on you, Norbus Clacknozzle, to conduct a Salt Melt on Azalea Clacknozzle, or whatever her real name is."

He nodded his head, and Rick and Tim placed a giant bag of salt at my feet. Dr. Grasmere wanted me to pour it on Azalea, because salt paralyzes zombies completely for twenty-four hours. After Azalea was melted, Dr. Grasmere would probably send her back to her own Territory. Or who knows what.

"You want me to Salt Melt Azalea? Right here, in front of everyone?"

Dr. Grasmere nodded solemnly. "The choices in battle are never easy ones."

I walked over to Azalea and put my hand on her shoulder. "Is it true? Are you really an Outsider?"

She refused to look at me. "Of course not," she whimpered. "I thought we were friends. I thought you cared about me."

"We ARE friends!" My voice was trembling, I could hear it, but I couldn't do anything about it. "I do care about you! And I trusted you! Was that all a lie?"

Her voice was barely above a whisper. "No! It's not true! I beg you, don't listen to them."

I could hear the afterlives all around me, talking to one another in disbelief. Azalea was a traitor. Could it be? I tried to gather my thoughts. I wanted to be the best Zombie Warrior ever; I wanted to make my country proud. I was being told that my podmate was a traitor, and I was being told to paralyze her. At the same time, I was having those weird flashbacks to my outside life, and something inside me was pulling me away from the zombie life, but I didn't know why. All I did know was that I had a decision to make.

I walked over to the bag of salt.

"Nooo!" cried Azalea. I moved closer to her. The bag was heavy, especially for a juvenile like myself. I dragged it across the circle, then tried to pick it up. Jim came over to help me, and Rick patted me on the back and said, "You've got this, kid." I think he was trying to make me feel better about what I was about to do, but he didn't. I felt awful.

Finally, I got the bag up to my shoulders. Azalea was looking at me with pure fear in her eyes. I glanced over quickly at Berstus and Frumpus, who looked like they would rather be anywhere else. Then I walked over to Azalea and leaned down so only she could hear me.

"I believe you," I said.

And then I walked over to Dr. Grasmere and dumped the bag of salt on his head.

"I *don't* believe you," I said.

He just stared at me, the salt falling from his body and gathering in a small mound at his feet.

I would say that all the afterlifes held their breath, but we don't breathe. Instead, everyone just stood perfectly still, frozen, waiting, staring at Dr. Grasmere. I glanced at Azalea—she still looked terrified, but also relieved, and very confused.

After five seconds, I turned back to Dr. Grasmere nervously. "I'm sorry," I said. "I couldn't do it. She's my friend."

He stared blankly, as if trying to decide what to do with me. "You have disappointed me greatly, Norbus," he said. "We have been training for this, and you didn't come through."

My mind whirled as I tried to process what was happening. "Training? You mean with the loud buzzing noises and the red lights? Don't you mean brainwashing?"

Dr. Grasmere's eyes narrowed into little slits. "It is clear that being on the outside has changed you. It has made you fantasize about being independent, a free thinker." He brushed off some of the salt that was still on his body. "I have news for you, Norbus. What you thought was salt was actually nothing more than finely crushed sand. Nothing would have happened to Azalea. This was just an exercise. A simulation to prove once and for all that you would make a fine Zombie Warrior, willing to make the hard decisions. It is clear we were mistaken."

He turned out to face the rest of the afterlifes, who were still watching our every move. "We know that some people who say they are our friends are really not our friends. Dr. Kinder, the woman who claims to be Norbus's adoptive mother, has turned completely against our program. She would like nothing more than to shut it down completely." Dr. Grasmere walked up to me. "We thought you were ready, Norbus. But you're not ready. You're not close to being ready." Then, surprisingly, he put his arm around my shoulder. "But I'm not angry. We're here to support you and help you learn. This is your home, after all, and there's no place like home. And you will stay, and you will continue to train, and learn. And if we have to intensify the training, we will."

"What does that mean?" I asked, but he ignored me. Instead, he nodded his head as if to give a signal, and the red light came back on. It seemed brighter and louder than ever. A giant screen appeared out of nowhere, with Commander Jensen's giant face on it. It seemed like he was staring straight at me. "Ring of Wisdom is over," he said.

"We have learned much here today." Then he raised both his arms to the sky, and everyone began to cheer. The buzzing started to blast through the speakers. Rick and Jim cheered, the staff cheered, the zombies cheered, even Azalea cheered. I glanced around, and everyone was yelling and cheering except for me and Sergeant Kelly, who stood completely still, staring straight ahead. She was always on duty.

Dr. Grasmere was watching me. "WHY AREN'T YOU CHEERING?" he yelled, trying to be heard above the noise. "DON'T YOU BELIEVE?" He pointed upward. "LOOK INTO THE LIGHT, NORBUS! ALL THE ANSWERS ARE IN THE LIGHT!"

But I didn't want to look into the light. I was done looking into the light, once and for all. I didn't want special training, and I realized I wasn't really home either. I closed my eyes. I covered my ears with my hands. I felt the red lights invade the darkness, but it wasn't nearly as bright. And the buzzing noise was getting softer . . . softer . . .

And the memories began flooding into my head, like always.

But this time, they were different memories.

I remembered running down the street after I escaped, lost and alone on the street, and the truck pulling up to me.

I remembered Mr. Kinder extending a hand.

Mrs. Kinder teaching me how to brush my teeth.

Lester making fun of me but protecting me.

Going to school, and meeting my friends.

Mrs. Kinder—my "mom"—tapping her chest and saying, *You'll always be right here.*

And suddenly I knew where I belonged.

I glanced up at my fellow zombies, who were all in a trance. Then I walked over to Dr. Grasmere.

"You're right," I told him. "There is no place like home."

But what I didn't tell him was that my home wasn't in here.

It was out there.

And I needed to go back.

PART IV
THE ESCAPE & THE RESCUE

OUTSIdE—FRIdAY, 4:14 P.M.

Evan

Lester looked like his eyes were going to pop out of his head.

"You want me to WHAT?!?!"

Kiki and I looked at each other. "I don't see why it's such a big deal," I said, trying to sound casual.

"You don't see why it's such a BIG DEAL?" Lester went back to polishing his bike, which is what he was doing when we told him our simple idea. "Evan, how long have we known each other?"

I was trying to figure out if this was some sort of a test. "Uh, about three months?"

"*Exactly.* Like, we barely know each other. So, why would you think I would even remotely entertain the idea of doing something like this?"

Kiki put her hand on Lester's arm. "Yeah, but you've known me a lot longer," she said. "We're, like, practically old friends. And besides, it's not like we're asking you to fly us to the moon or anything, right?"

Lester threw his rag down on the seat and glared at us. "You want me to break into a government facility! And then break someone OUT of that very same government facility! That's (a) crazy, (b) nuts, and (c) totally insane." He picked the rag back up and started twirling it nervously in his hand. "Oh yeah, and (d) completely bonkers. Forget it."

"I can't believe you, Lester," I said. "You're Arnold's brother! They tricked him to get him to go back there, and you went and visited him and saw how they, like, brainwashed him—"

"Zombies don't have brains," interrupted Lester.

"Yes they do," Kiki said. "They don't *eat* brains, but they definitely have them."

Lester rolled his eyes. "Whatever. The answer is no. And besides, my parents are figuring it all out."

Kiki shook her head. "The last time they figured it all out, Arnold got sent back."

"I can't help you." Lester turned his music back on. We were just about to give up and walk away, when our secret weapon walked up.

Otherwise known as Darlene.

"What's up, youngsters?" she said, fist-bumping each of us. "Helping Lester shine up his bike for like the tenth time this week?"

Lester took his earbuds out just in time to hear Darlene make fun of him. "Ha-ha-ha," he said, not very enthusiastically. "They were just leaving."

Kiki and I looked at each other, as if we both had the same idea at the same time. Kiki spoke first. "Actually, Darlene, can we ask you something? It's about Arnold."

"No way," Lester said, but we weren't listening.

"What about him?" Darlene said. "Jeez, I sure do miss that little guy."

"Us, too," I said. "We miss him a lot. But he's stuck in that terrible place he called the Territory, and they're not letting him out."

Darlene sighed. "I know, I know. You think they're going to keep him like, another week or something?"

"I think they're going to keep him forever," I said. "I don't think we'll ever see Arnold again."

"Hey, wait a second," Lester said. "Nobody ever said anything about that. They just need him for a little while longer—that's what that doctor said."

"I asked my dad about it, Lester," I said. "He doesn't think they're ever going to let him out. He thinks they're just saying that so the Kinders won't freak out."

Lester looked like he'd eaten an overripe banana. "Oh man. That's not good."

"I'll say it's not good!" Darlene put one of her big boots on the back of Lester's bike, right where he'd been cleaning, which didn't make him happy. "What are we gonna do about it?"

"My parents are figuring it out with Evan's dad," Lester said. "I think they're going to write a letter to some lawyer they know in the government."

"A lawyer in the government?" asked Darlene. "First of all, that sounds complicated. And second of all, isn't the government the one who runs that program in the first place?"

Lester was starting to look uncomfortable. "Well, yeah, but . . ." he said, trailing off.

Darlene twirled a strand of her pink hair. "But, what?"

I wanted to jump in, and it seemed like the right time. "We want to break Arnold out," I said.

Darlene whipped her head around. "You want to *what*?"

"Break Arnold out," Kiki said. "You know, rescue him. Help him escape."

Darlene let out a long, low whistle. "Wow, dudes. That is just . . . what's the word I'm looking for . . . oh yeah. Nutso."

"I know, right??" Lester agreed, looking a little relieved.

A wicked grin crossed Darlene's face. "Totally nutso, and I love it."

Lester dropped his rag. "You what?"

"I LOVE it." Darlene sat down in the grass. "So what's the plan?"

"That's what we were just talking to Lester about," Kiki said, winking at him. "You've been there, so you would know how to find it again, right?"

"I guess," he said glumly. Just because he was grateful for us helping him look good in front of his girlfriend didn't mean he was suddenly all gung ho about breaking into a government installation. "I mean, I remember the town where it was, and I could probably figure it out once we got there. But yo, there's just one small problem: I'm too young to drive, remember?"

Darlene grinned. "Isn't that why God invented car services?"

"Oh, right," mumbled Lester.

Darlene jumped to her feet and kissed Lester right on the mouth. Kiki and I stared. It was the first mouth-to-mouth kiss I'd ever seen up close. I didn't realize something could be so gross and so awesome at the same time.

It turns out, though, that one kiss has a lot of power. Lester suddenly adopted a take-charge attitude. "So here's what we're going to do," he said. "Tomorrow, we're going to tell our parents that we're going hiking for the day, and that we need money for lunch and dinner. Then we're going to get a taxi and drive down to the town where the Territory is. Then we're going to sneak in, find Arnold, and grab him." He paused and took a deep breath. "And then we're going to run as fast as we can."

As soon as he was finished talking, Darlene, Kiki, and I all did the same thing. We cheered.

"This will either be the awesomest thing we ever do, or the dumbest," Lester added. "But I guess we won't know which until we do it."

"My friend has an older brother named Simon who works for one of those driving companies," Darlene said. "I'll ask him to take us."

Lester nodded. "Tell him it's a round-trip. And the cab has to be big enough for five of us, since we'll have Arnold with us on the way home."

"Actually, six of us," I said.

Lester and Darlene looked at me and both said, "Huh?"

"Six of us," I repeated. "There's someone else who needs to come."

"What we're doing is dangerous," said Lester. "No

one else can know. Why would you want to bring another person?"

Kiki and I looked at each other.

"Because we wouldn't be doing it if it weren't for her," Kiki said.

INSIdE—FRIdAY, 5:32 P.M.

Arnold

I kept to myself for the rest of the night after the Ring of Wisdom. Now that I'd made up my mind to try and escape, I wanted to be alone, to see if I could bring up any more memories about life outside. I knew they were buried somewhere inside my head, and I knew that they'd actually happened, but the deprogramming I'd gone through was powerful and the memories would only come in quick glimpses. I wanted more.

The next day, I tried to act like everything was normal. During Morning Exercise Circle, I even cheered when the red light came on. Later, after dinner, I was walking back to the pod when Frumpus and Berstus came up beside me, so quickly that I didn't have time to sneak away.

"You were very courageous last night, to not Salt Melt Azalea," Frumpus said. "I don't care what Dr. Grasmere says, I think you are a true Zombie Warrior."

Berstus was shaking his head. "That wasn't very nice, what they put Azalea through."

"The poor thing was scared to death," I said. "It was a dirty trick."

"A dirty trick how?" asked Frumpus.

"The way they build up our trust and then tear it down. It's not right."

"Who's 'they'?" asked Berstus.

"Everyone here. The humans who designed us, and created us, and built us." I stopped walking and looked at them. "You both realize that, right?"

They both looked completely lost and confused. "I don't know what you're talking about," Frumpus said.

I opened my arms wide. "This whole place! It's a project, and we're the subjects. Which is why they call us 'subjects.' We're experiments, who were originally created to attack America so society could unite over destroying us. Now they want us to join *their* military and spy on people they think are threatening the American way of life."

"How do you know all this?" Berstus asked.

I could feel the cold blood in my body rushing to my head as I got more and more upset. "The better question is, how do you NOT know all this? Because of how you've been programmed, that's how. Every time they turn on those red lights and start to play that loud buzzing sound through the loudspeakers, that's when they're programming us, or deprogramming us. They're placing or replacing information inside our brains."

They both stopped walking. "I don't understand," Berstus said.

"We're not real," I said. "We're science projects. It's one thing to not be human. But it's another to not be treated humanely. I want to go where I will be treated humanely."

Frumpus bent down to look me in the eye. "What are you saying, Norbus?"

I started walking again, worried I'd said too much. "Nothing. It's just . . . it's something that we should all want, that's all."

"Do you think . . ." Frumpus said, then stopped. "Do you

think there's a place out there for us? A place like where you were?"

"I don't know," I told them honestly. "I hope so. That's why I agreed to come here in the first place, to make sure that could happen. But now we all know that was a lie."

"A lie," Berstus repeated, like the word was part of a foreign language.

"We didn't choose to become part of this world," I told them. "That choice was made for us. But now that we're here, we deserve to be treated just like everyone else. No better, no worse—just the same."

Berstus and Frumpus both nodded but didn't say anything. We walked silently for a few minutes, as if all imagining a better, more fair world. But then we rounded the corner and arrived at our pod, and they stopped short. Their faces went dark.

"What is it?" I asked. "What's wrong?" They glanced at each other, but neither one spoke. I shrugged. "Okay, fine, I'll be the only talkative one."

I opened the door to the pod and stepped inside. Standing there were Dr. Grasmere and Sergeant Kelly. Azalea was sitting between them, staring at the floor.

"We've been waiting for you," Dr. Grasmere said. His ever-present politeness was nowhere to be found. He was done playing nice. This time, he was playing for keeps.

"I don't understand," I said. "I was just coming in to get ready for Nighttime Lecture."

"Oh, were you, now?" Dr. Grasmere pulled out a tape recorder and pressed play. I heard my own voice. *That's why I agreed to come here in the first place, to make sure that could happen. But now we all know that was a lie.*

Dr. Grasmere laughed without smiling. "Did you actually think we didn't listen in to every word you said? Did you actually think we didn't monitor every move you make? What kind of scientists would we be if we didn't keep an eye on our subjects, every second of every day? Poor ones, I'd say." He nodded at Sergeant Kelly. "Let's wrap this up, shall we? Sergeant Kelly, please bring Subject 48356 to my office, where we will begin Isolation Therapy."

Sergeant Kelly moved toward me. She had a sad expression in her eyes but was moving toward me with purpose, and I had about three seconds to decide what to do next. Would I accept my fate, or would I take a chance? Would I surrender, or would I fight?

"Run, Norbus!" Azalea said suddenly. "Run back to your family!"

Dr. Grasmere looked down at Azalea, then at Sergeant Kelly. "Sergeant, please take this subject to Isolation

Therapy as well," he said, but before anyone moved, I Zombie Zing'd Sergeant Kelly right on the neck. She froze in place instantly.

And then, before Dr. Grasmere even realized what was happening, I ran. I bolted out of the tent as fast as my rubbery legs would take me. Sergeant Kelly couldn't run after me, of course. Dr. Grasmere made a quick phone call to a staff member. "Don't harm him in any way!" I heard him yell. "Make sure you take him alive!"

Even in my highly stressed state, I could appreciate the irony in that.

If only I *were* alive.

INSIdE—FRIdAY, 5:48 P.M.

Arnold

I rounded the corner outside the pod and ran to the large building we used for Morning Routine. I knew it would only be a matter of minutes before Dr. Grasmere got either Berstus or Frumpus to undo the Zombie Zing on Sergeant Kelly, and they would be after me, along with pretty much the entire staff of the Territory. But I had one advantage over them.

I was a zombie.

I couldn't run fast, and I couldn't throw a ball to save my life (if I'd had a life), but I was as elastic as a rubber band. Which meant I could slip between cracks in walls, slide underneath holes in fences, and shimmy my way through the narrowest of spaces.

I had one destination in mind: the Outer Fence. The Outer Fence is where I'd originally escaped, and if I could just get back to the area where we'd dug the tunnel, I might be able to slip underneath, just like last time. Unfortunately, the Outer Fence was clear across campus. I ran as fast as I could (which wasn't very fast) for a few minutes, then turned a corner and stopped short. The place was crawling with soldiers, all looking for me. The realization hit me hard: One zombie was no match for the might of the National Martial Services.

I sunk down to the ground grimly, wondering how I would ever get back to the Kinders, when I noticed a building in front of me that I'd never seen before. It was tucked away and hard to notice, because its dark green color blended in with the trees around it. Across the front of it were two words written in small gold lettering: THE INFIRMARY.

As soon as I saw those words, I knew I had I seen them before. But where? It took me a few seconds, and then it came to me: They were written on the boxes that we'd unloaded from the truck. The boxes that had our "weapons" in them, which turned out to be nothing more than a small green pill.

And I remembered something else: That pill had been called The Strength, and allowed us to get across a giant field in a single step and reach the roof of a building in a single jump. It had the weird side effects afterward, of course, but I decided not to think about that.

Instead I thought, *Wait a second. What if there were more of those pills somewhere inside the Infirmary?*

I realized that there might be a way home after all.

OUTSIDE—FRIDAY, 6:19 P.M.

Evan

So it turns out that Sarah Anne has a really funny laugh.

When Kiki and I went over to her house to talk about rescuing Arnold, the first thing that happened was we met her mom. She was really nice and a little stunned that Sarah Anne suddenly had friends visiting her. She'd met Kiki, but seeing me was a whole new level of shock—her daughter had a gang!

If only she knew that we were planning to take her daughter with us on a dangerous mission.

After finishing up the incredible snack spread that Sarah Anne's mom had laid out, we went downstairs to her basement, where it was our turn to be shocked. Sarah Anne had set it up to look like mission control at a space station. There were chairs, computers, charts, and maps. Sarah Anne sat in front of a computer and didn't say anything. She just started typing—fast.

After a minute, Kiki said, "Um, what are you typing?"

Sarah Anne didn't look up or even acknowledge Kiki—she just stayed focused on the computer. After five minutes, Sarah pushed her chair back from the desk. Kiki and I leaned in to read what she'd written.

THE PLAN TO RESCUE ARNOLD Z. OMBEE.

Government Territory 278 is thirty-seven miles from here.

The lab operates twenty-four hours a day, with military personnel guarding the gatehouse at all times.

Satellite images from Google Earth show a compound of seven buildings, which form a giant rectangle. In the center is a field, or training ground.

There is one building that is hidden away in the woods. The internet doesn't say what that building is called, but it's green and has a square shape with a short wing on each side. Behind that building are some woods that drop down to a stream. This will be our point of entrance—it is the only place on the compound that is not surrounded with barbed wire, because zombies can't swim.

A car will drop us half a mile up the road. Then we will have to walk the remainder of the way. We will disembark the car before dawn, so by the time we get to the Territory, it will be just light enough to see but dark enough to still have some cover. Three of us will set out to find Arnold. Also, I have bought orange jumpsuits at the mall for all of us, because that's what Arnold told us zombies wear in the Territory. This way we can blend in. I told my mom they were for a school play. But for some reason, if anyone figures out who we are, we will pretend to be students who got lost on a field trip. Meanwhile, two of us will stay in the car, waiting for a prearranged signal to announce that we have Arnold; they will then meet us by the road outside the clearing.

Tomorrow morning's weather conditions will be favorable, with fog limiting visibility and the possibility of rain to slow down pursuers.

After we read it, Kiki and I just looked at each other for about ten seconds. Finally I said, "This is the most awesome thing I've ever seen."

"That goes double for me," Kiki said.

And that's when Sarah Anne let out that amazing laugh. She didn't need her letter board, and neither did we. We just all gave the thumbs-up sign. We were a go.

INSIdE—FRIdAY, 9:18 P.M.

Arnold

I kept an eye on the Infirmary, watching as people came and went. Finally, I decided to hunker down in the woods until the middle of the night, when hopefully the building would basically be empty. Meanwhile I could hear the search going on above me. There were soldiers running by, and I could hear jeeps and other vehicles racing around. At one point, there was even a helicopter hovering overhead, sweeping the campus. But I was dug in well, and for the first five or so hours, no one found me.

I was feeling confident about my chances to make it through the night, when I saw a flashlight pierce the darkness. It was pointing straight over my head.

"He's around here somewhere," a voice said. "He's got to be. The dogs have picked up his scent."

I was confused for a second, because I knew that zombies have no smell. But then I remembered: *sudoris zombutam*.

Zombie sweat.

The one time we do exude an odor is when we're stressed out. That's when we release the sticky, gooey substance known as zombie sweat. According to Dr. Grasmere, it is one of the most stinkiest stinks known to man. I wouldn't know, because we don't have a sense of smell, but when I looked down at my feet, I could see the telltale yellow goo seeping out the sides of my shoes.

Uh-oh.

I'm sure that's what the dogs were tracking. It was going to be only a matter of moments before they locked in on my exact location. The flashlight was getting closer. I could hear the dogs barking more and more furiously.

I made a spur-of-the-moment decision.

A few hundred feet away was the door to the Infirmary. It was locked, but earlier in the night, I'd watched as people punched a key code to gain entry. I'd memorized the code: 121261. By my calculations, I could make it up to the building, punch in the code, and slip into the building in forty-eight seconds, which might be just enough time to get there before the search party made it out into the clearing.

I made a break for it.

My shoes squeaked with sweat as I scampered up to the building as fast as my rubber-band legs could carry me. I punched in the code and heard the door lock release with a *click!* It was the sweetest sound I'd ever heard.

The building was deserted and pitch-black, which was perfect. I looked at a clock on the wall: 4:48 a.m. I had two hours before daylight, when the first workers would arrive for the day. Two hours to search the building without being noticed. Two hours to find the pill that would hopefully change my life.

Well, semi-life, anyway.

OUTSIDE—FRIDAY, 7:12 P.M.—SATURDAY, 4:38 A.M.

Evan

The night before, I got a text from Lester with the details:

Driver is Simon.
pick U up in Honda Odyssey Minivan
C U @ 4:30 a.m.
BRIGHT AND EARLY!!!

It was getting real.

As I ate dinner with my parents, it felt like they were staring at me nonstop, examining me for any signs that I might be planning something crazy (which of course I was). I was sure I was imagining it until dessert, when my dad said, "So, have you been thinking about Arnold a lot?"

I nearly spit out my gluten-free, fat-free, taste-free

frozen yogurt. (I guess *dessert* is an exaggeration.)

"What—what do you mean?"

My dad lowered his fork. "Well, I mean, are you sad? Do you miss him? I'm helping the Kinders set up some meetings with lawyers for next week. Our goal is still to get him back, of course."

You and me both, I thought, *but I think I'm one step ahead of ya.*

"That's great, Dad." I managed another bite before coming up with a suitable change of subject. "Mrs. Huggle thinks my math grade is going to go way up this quarter," I announced. "She's really impressed with my progress."

"That's wonderful, Evan," said my mom, who didn't eat dessert, even though I knew she had a secret stash of chocolate chip cookies in the back of the cabinet. (I helped myself on occasion, but she never knew.) "But we really want to know how you're feeling. Having a friend in trouble can be very difficult, and we just want to make sure that you're okay, and if you want to talk about it with us, you can."

"Got it, thanks." I got up from the table with what I hoped was a calm, natural motion but was probably the opposite of that. "Well, I'm really tired, and I have some homework, so I'm going to go up to my room and do that homework, and then probably just go to bed, because I'm really tired—did I mention that already?"

I know—smooth, right?

"Okay, honey," said my mom, looking at me for what seemed like a few extra seconds. "We'll be up in a bit to say good night."

"Okay, but I might be asleep."

"I'm very glad you're taking care of yourself, Evan," said my dad. "It's so important to get enough sleep, especially at your age."

That seemed like a bad time to mention that I was getting up in the middle of the night to try and rescue my friend from Government Territory 278, so I didn't.

😵 😎 😄

The next morning, my alarm went off at four o'clock, but it didn't have to, because I was already up. Ten minutes later, I was dressed, downstairs, and ready to go. My parents were upstairs sleeping peacefully. If everything went according to plan, we might even be back before they knew I was missing!

That was a big *if*, of course, but I didn't want to think about that part.

At exactly 4:33, a pair of headlights pulled into my street and parked in front of the house next to ours. That was the signal. I hustled outside, ran to the van, and pulled the door open. Lester, Darlene, and Kiki were already there.

"Good morning, everyone!" I said, as cheerfully as possible, before I realized that Lester and Darlene were both asleep.

"Good morning," whispered Kiki. "Can you believe this is happening?"

"Not really," I said. "Where's Sarah Anne?"

"We're going to pick her up now." Kiki pointed at Lester and Darlene. "Look at these two. How can they sleep at a time like this?"

I shrugged. "My mom always said teenagers can sleep through anything, and this proves it."

The driver turned around. "How's it going, I'm Simon," he said.

"Nice to meet you, Simon. Please drive carefully." Uh-oh, I was starting to sound like my mom.

We drove about ten minutes through the dark before pulling up across the street from Sarah Anne's house. Her house was pitch-black, and we couldn't see anything. After about twenty seconds of silence, I was about to ask Kiki what to do, when there was a light tap on the door. For some reason, that woke Lester up. He pulled the door open, and Sarah Anne hopped in, clutching her letter board and a pink backpack.

"What's in the backpack?" Lester asked. "Oh, and hey, I'm Lester."

"This is Sar—" I started to say, before Sarah Anne put her hand on my arm to stop me. She reached for her letter board and her hands started flying. I realized there was no way Lester would be able to follow her, so I translated.

"MY NAME IS SARAH ANNE. THANK YOU FOR HELPING US."

"Uh, you're welcome," Lester said.

"AND I BROUGHT SNACKS."

Darlene opened her eyes at the word *snacks*.

"Hey, you must be Sarah Anne," she mumbled. "I'm Darlene. Snacks. Cool." Then she closed her eyes again.

Sarah Anne almost never made eye contact with anyone, but for the first time ever, I saw her shoulders relax just a little bit. She sat back in her seat, took a deep breath, then looked out the window.

Simon reached back and pulled the van door shut.

"We should be there in about forty minutes," he said.

INSIdE—SATURdAY, 5:28 A.m.

Arnold

The inside of the Infirmary brought back a quick flash memory—a nurse's office somewhere, a few human children and me lying in beds, and a nice nurse taking care of us. I suddenly remembered her name: Nurse Raposo. The Infirmary reminded me of her room at school, but about a thousand times bigger and more intense.

There were a bunch of rooms with hospital beds in them, and a bunch of other rooms with laboratory equipment in them, and still more rooms with chairs, and blackboards, and skeletons, and charts of the human body.

But the odd thing was, there were no actual people anywhere. Even though it was around five-thirty in the morning, I still would have expected to see security people or custodial workers, but there was no one. There were a few lights on, and cameras everywhere, but no actual people.

After about ten minutes of exploring and trying to figure out where I might find the pill I needed, I suddenly heard voices. They were very distant, but after a few seconds, I could tell they were getting closer. I needed to move, to find someplace to hide. I ran around a corner and saw a room with a black door. On the door were written the words CRANIAL INSERTION.

My cold blood started running even colder.

CRANIAL INSERTION.

Meaning, that was where they put the brains in.

That was the moment I realized exactly what that room was, and what the whole building was. My brain buzzed with an uneasy feeling of what humans call déjà vu. Meaning, I knew I'd been there before.

The Infirmary was where Project Z was implemented.

Where the plan was executed.

Where I was created.

Maybe that was why the building was virtually empty. Because all the zombies were already made!

I ran up to the black door and tried it. Amazingly enough, it was unlocked. I went inside. There was one dark purple light on, just enough for me to make out what was in there. There was a long steel table in the middle of the room, with a giant unlit light looming above it. I stared, trying to imagine myself lying on that table, with Dr. Grasmere putting a brain inside my reanimated body.

I thought, *This is where I began.*

I closed my eyes and waited for the voices in the hall to pass by. When they got in front of the room, though, the voices stopped. I looked underneath the door and could see shadows. They weren't moving. Then the voices started up again. I tiptoed closer to the door, to see if I could hear what they were saying, but I could only make out a few words here and there.

"...inside the cerebral cortex," one voice said. "...higher level of anger response."

"... can examine in the next phase," another voice said.

There was a pause, and then I heard a third voice, loud

and clear. "There won't be a next phase unless we find the missing subject."

They were talking about me.

The shadows finally moved away. I waited another minute, then slowly opened the door and peeked down the hall. No one was there. I made my way to the stairwell, where there was a directory that listed all the rooms in the building. I scanned it quickly until I found what I was looking for.

ROOM 207: PHARMACY.

If the pill they called The Strength was going to be anywhere, it would be there.

I headed up the stairs.

OUTSIDE—SATURDAY, 6:38 A.M.

Evan

"This is it," our driver Simon announced. "This is where you wanted me to stop, right? Mile marker 1402, right outside Danklin County?"

We all looked at Sarah Anne, who nodded.

"This is it," said Lester.

I took maybe the deepest breath I've ever taken. "Okay," I said. "I have to say something. I know we said that three of us would walk to the Territory, and two of us would stay behind. And I'm sure you guys all think that I should be one of the people who stay behind, on account of my leg and all. But I just want to say that I really, really want to be one of the people that go. Because I'm, you know, kind of Arnold's first and best friend, you know, of his human friends, not including his family of course, and so I think I should be there when we rescue him." I paused for a second, then added, "Which we're definitely going to do."

The others looked at one another for a second, neither of them quite sure what to say. Then Lester said, "So, Evan, let me ask you something. How fast can you walk in that thing?"

"'That thing'?" said Darlene. "That is so not cool, Lester."

"Okay, okay, sorry," Lester muttered. "So how fast can you walk with that, uh, leg? And more to the point, how fast can you run?"

"Fast," I said, trying to sound like I meant it. "Definitely fast enough."

Lester scrunched up his eyes in thought for a few seconds. "Okay," he said. "It will be me, you, and Kiki. Darlene and Sarah Anne, you guys will wait here for us, okay?"

"Are you sure?" Kiki asked. "Sarah Anne, do you want to go?"

We all looked at Sarah Anne, but she kept looking out the window. She wasn't great at eye contact. After a few seconds, she shook her head, handed me the map she had downloaded off the internet, then reached for her board. BRING HIM BACK SAFE.

"You bet," I said.

We went over all the preparations one last time: If

Sarah Anne's calculations were correct, we would reach the stream behind the square building in about twelve minutes. We would have approximately seven minutes to make it across the stream, and then twenty minutes to look for Arnold before it was light out. If we found him, we would call Darlene immediately to tell her we were on our way back, since we were pretty sure there would be no cell service in the woods. They'd be exactly where we left them, the car would be running, off we'd go, and everyone would be safe and sound.

That was the plan, anyway.

Lester, Kiki, and I slid open the van door, which sounded really loud in the predawn silence. We got outside and put the orange jumpsuits on over our clothes. Then we waved good-bye to Sarah Anne and Darlene and headed off into the woods.

INSIDE—SATURDAY, 6:37 A.M.

Arnold

The second floor was dark and deserted. I quickly spotted room 207, which was three doors down on the left. I scampered over to the door and turned the knob.

It was locked.

I tried to peer in, but the door had the kind of frosted glass on it that makes it hard to see anything. I could see a lot of shelves with boxes on them. I just couldn't read the labels on the boxes.

I hesitated.

The way I saw it, I had two choices: Sneak back out of the building without being caught, try to run back into the woods without being seen, and come up with a whole new plan that probably wouldn't work. Or I could break the glass on the door, probably set off some sort of alarm, and hope that I'd find the pill before security made their way upstairs.

I chose B.

I closed my eyes for a second, then threw my elbow against the glass part of the door. There was a soft *thwack!* but the glass didn't budge. I tried again, but the same thing happened.

Oh, right, I said to myself. *I'm incredibly weak. I almost forgot that part.*

I decided to try one last time. I walked quietly down the hall, turned around, took a deep breath, and went charging toward the door as fast as my little zombie legs would carry me. When I got to the door, I kicked my leg up over my head—we're really flexible, remember?—and slammed my foot into the glass.

This time, it shattered.

Actually, the glass didn't just shatter. It *SHATTERED*. Shards went flying everywhere, with a sound that was way louder than I was expecting. (If I were a human person, I definitely would have been nervous about getting cut by the glass, but I didn't have to worry about that. See? There *are* advantages to being a zombie.) There was no way someone wasn't going to hear it. I had to move fast. I reached through the broken glass, unlocked the door from the inside, and went into the room. I immediately started tearing through the boxes and examining the labels—since zombies can read really fast, it only took me about five seconds to go through all the shelves in the room. I saw boxes labeled BLOOD TRANSFER STATION, X-RAY GOGGLES, and RED STREAK DYE, but no sign of THE STRENGTH.

I heard footsteps again. But this time, they were accompanied by yelling, and I knew whoever it was, was coming straight for me.

I glanced around, maybe looking for a window to jump out of (I was on the second floor, so I'm pretty sure that jump wouldn't have gone very well), when I saw one last shelf, behind a large wooden table.

It said T.S. 147: TEST PHASE.

Could T.S. *mean The Strength?*

I ran to the box and ripped it open. Tons of small containers spilled out, each holding one small green pill.

Yes!

The footsteps were getting closer. I heard a voice yell, "THERE! 207!"

I grabbed a single container, left the room, and went out into the hall. I saw four soldiers headed my way. They saw me and pointed.

"STOP!" yelled one soldier. "DON'T TAKE ANOTHER STEP!"

I did stop. But then I took the pill out of the container, put it in my mouth, and swallowed.

I heard a second soldier say, "What the heck is he doing?" and a third soldier say, "Put your arms in the air."

I didn't wait for the fourth solider to say anything. Instead, I took a single step and flew past them down the hall so quickly I could barely register their shocked eyes. A second step got me down the entire flight of stairs. A third step got me to the front door. I pulled at the knob, and the entire door came off in my hands. I threw the door down just in time to see a bunch of cars and jeeps turning into the driveway of the Infirmary. Their horns were blaring. Dr. Grasmere jumped out of the first jeep.

"WAIT, NORBUS!" he yelled. "I know you took a pill! Please don't do anything further! Come talk to me! You have to trust me!" He paused, then yelled even louder, "YOU HAVE TO TRUST ME!"

I looked at him. Then I looked at all the other soldiers, who were hopping out of their cars and jeeps, guns pointed straight at me. Did they think they were going to shoot me and kill me? Didn't they know you couldn't kill someone who wasn't really alive?

"BUT THAT'S THE PROBLEM," I yelled back to Dr. Grasmere. "I *DID* TRUST YOU."

"WAIT!" he yelled again, more desperately.

But I was done waiting. I was done waiting, and hoping, and helping.

I jumped.

OUTSIdE—SATURdAY, 6:52 A.M.

Evan

We made it to the stream in thirteen minutes. I probably cost us the extra minute. Lester and Kiki were a little ahead of me, but I was doing a pretty good job keeping up. For the first five minutes, Kiki kept turning around and asking, "Evan, are you okay?" Finally I said, "If you ask me that again, I'll tell everyone at school you still sleep with the light on and the door open." That got her to be quiet.

The stream turned out to be more like a river. It wasn't very wide, but it had a real current to it and was rushing pretty fast. There was no way to know how deep it was, but we all assumed there would be some swimming involved, which wasn't going to be all that easy with clothes and a jumpsuit on. Across the way, we could just make out a shadow of the building we were looking for. There were some lights on, and we could see some headlights, meaning cars were there.

"That's weird," Lester said. "What the heck could be going on there at this time of night?"

"This time of morning, you mean," I said.

"Whatever," Lester said, and he had a point.

Kiki peered into the distance. "Yeah, that is weird. It's almost like there's some sort of meeting going on."

Suddenly, we could hear voices. Loud voices.

"YOU HAVE TO TRUST ME!" the first voice said.

We all looked at one another.

"Wait a second, was that that guy, Dr. Grasmere?" Lester asked. "I met that guy."

Before Kiki or I could answer, we heard another, unmistakable voice.

"BUT THAT'S THE PROBLEM. I *DID* TRUST YOU."

We all looked at one another. *Arnold!*

We heard Dr. Grasmere yell, "WAIT!" There was about a five-second pause. And then, just as dawn was breaking enough for us to see it completely clearly, we saw someone who looked a lot like our friend Arnold Z. Ombee shooting up into the sky and landing in a tree-top, about two hundred yards above the earth.

We all stood there, for about fifteen seconds, trying to absorb what we'd just seen.

And then we all jumped in the river and started swimming as fast as we could.

INSIdE—SATURdAY, 7:07 A.M.

Arnold

It's a lot windier sitting on the top of a tree than it is standing on earth.

That was one of the first things I realized as I clung to a branch and looked down at all the people below. They looked more like tiny insects.

I could tell which one was Dr. Grasmere, though, because he wearing that red jacket he liked. He was scurrying around, but I couldn't tell why. Then I heard his voice coming through some sort of machine.

"NORBUS, THIS IS DR. GRASMERE. I KNOW YOU CAN BARELY SEE ME, BUT I'M SPEAKING THROUGH A MEGAPHONE, SO I HOPE YOU CAN HEAR ME. YOU ARE IN DANGER. YOU'LL REMEMBER THAT WE HAVEN'T WORKED OUT THE KINKS OF THE STRENGTH YET. IN A MATTER OF MINUTES, YOU WILL NOT BE ABLE TO CONTROL YOUR BODY AND YOU WILL COME CRASHING DOWN! IT'S POSSIBLE YOUR BODY COULD DISINTEGRATE

ON CONTACT." He paused for a second to let that sink in. "NORBUS, PLEASE wave your arms IF YOU CAN HEAR ME!"

"My name's not Norbus," I muttered to myself. "It's Arnold."

But I waved my arms anyway.

"GOOD! GOOD! PLEASE COME DOWN FROM THERE AND WE CAN FIGURE OUT WHERE TO GO FROM HERE."

I was deciding what to do, when I noticed shadows moving in the river behind the building.

INSIdE — SATURdAY, 7:09 A.m.

Evan

The river turned out to be pretty deep, but it wasn't wide at all, and we made it across in about three minutes. We all sat on the other side for a few seconds, catching our breath and trying to wring out our clothes (which didn't work very well).

"Sarah Anne said there was a brick building on the middle of campus that looked like housing," I said. "Let's head there."

Kiki looked down at her map. "It's this way."

We started plowing through the thick brush on the bank of the river and made our way up to a dirt road. There were a few jeeps driving very slowly, and in the distance, we saw people walking alongside the road. They had the slow, slightly lopsided walk that Arnold had.

"Holy smokes," Lester whispered.

I glanced over at him. "Holy smokes what?"

"Holy smokes, those are all zombies."

"Whoa," Kiki said.

We crept a little closer, still hugging close to the tree line so we couldn't be seen. I realized Lester was absolutely right. It looked like there were about thirty of them, they were all wearing the jumpsuits, and they all had the lopsided shuffle that Arnold had.

I elbowed Kiki in the ribs. "What should we do?"

But Lester answered. "Let's ask them how to get to where Arnold is."

Kiki and I looked at each other.

"You guys got a better idea?" Lester asked.

Uh, no we didn't.

"Kiki, you do the talking," Lester said, apparently realizing that talking about talking to zombies was one thing, but actually talking to them was another.

"Okay," Kiki said. She always was the bravest person I knew, and that proved it.

We quickly walked over to the zombies and fell in line like we belonged. They all seemed to be large and adult-size, except for one girl. "Let's talk to her," I suggested, and Kiki nodded her agreement.

We approached her as quickly and quietly as we could. "Excuse me," Kiki said. The girl turned her head, and her eyes went wide with shock. All the other zombies noticed us, too, and seemed similarly surprised. I got the feeling they weren't fooled by the orange jumpsuits.

"Excuse me," Kiki repeated. "Do you know an Arnold Z. Ombee?"

"Ar—Arnold who?"

"Arnold Z. Ombee." Kiki fished a picture of Arnold out of her pocket—she took it after school one day when we were walking home, I was in the picture, too, but I looked terrible—and showed it to the zombie girl. "This is what he looks like."

"Yes, I know him," the girl zombie whispered.

"We just saw something terrible happen to him," I whispered. "He got shot out of cannon into a tree! We need to help him!"

But before I could get any more information out of the girl, an adult zombie walked up to us and protectively shielded the child behind her. She stared at us. "What is happening here? Are you . . . are you human children?"

"Of course not!" Lester said. "We're totally zombies, like you guys."

"Why are you wet?" the adult demanded.

Well, it turns out one question was all it took. Lester's shoulders sagged. "Okay, fine, we're human. But don't tell, okay? We need to find our buddy!"

The adult looked around, as if to make sure she wasn't being watched. Then she leaned in and said, "We know Arnold. His name is Norbus here."

Kiki burst out laughing before she could catch herself. "NORBUS? Are you SERIOUS?"

It was a funny name, she was right about that—but unfortunately her laughter caught the attention of someone we hadn't noticed before—a human woman who was at the front of the line of zombies. She was dressed like a soldier, which meant she probably *was* a soldier. I was pretty sure they didn't play dress-up in the Territory.

The soldier woman starting walking over to us.

"Uh-oh," said Lester.

Just before the soldier reached us, the young zombie girl told us one last, very important thing.

"Your friend is in the tree because he's trying to go home," she said.

INSIdE—SATURdAY, 7:11 A.m.

Arnold

After a few more seconds, I could tell that the shadows were actually three shapes. They looked like humans, and they looked like they had emerged from the river. I thought maybe my eyes were playing tricks on me since the shapes were so far away, but there was something about them that looked familiar. Then I saw them walk over to group of afterlifes who were probably heading to breakfast. The whole thing was very confusing. It's hard to tell what's going on when everyone looks like ants.

It was clear, however, that the new ants were slightly smaller ants than the other ants.

INSIdE—SATURdAY, 7:12 A.m.

Evan

The soldier had a gun, but she wasn't pointing it at us. Instead, she had a look of concern on her face, like she thought we were in trouble.

I probably would have thought that, too, if I were her.

"What are you doing here? What do you want? Why are you wearing those jumpsuits, and why are you wet?" She could tell how nervous we were, since all of our knees were shaking audibly. "Okay, okay, no need to be so scared. You're a long way from where you're supposed to be. Haven't you kids heard of Google Maps? Or are you running away?"

"We're on a field trip," I mumbled, realizing how ridiculous it sounded as soon as I said it.

The soldier smirked. "Well, I'd like to know what kind of school you go to—because it's seven in the morning, and you happen to be trespassing on government property."

That perked Lester up. "Wait, we're on government property? Cool."

The soldier's face got suddenly stern. "You think this is cool?" she demanded.

Lester turned white. "No, ma'am," he trembled.

"You've broken the law."

"Yes, ma'am."

Her face softened just as quickly as it had hardened. "Wow, pranks have gotten a lot crazier since when I was your age. What are your names?" said the soldier. "The sooner you identify yourselves, the sooner we can sort this out and get you kids back home to your parents. And there are going to be some higher-ups who want to know how you knew about the jumpsuits." The soldier shook her head. "I don't imagine that's going to go over so well."

The three of us looked at one another for a few seconds—which, apparently, were a few seconds longer than the soldier thought was ideal. "Kids! I need you to tell me who you are now, please," she said, using her firm voice again. "I don't want any of you to get in more trouble than you're already in."

I decided, for once in my life, to be first. "My name is Evan Brantley. My father used to work here, as regional commander of the National Martial Services. We came here to rescue one of your subjects, Arnold Z. Ombee, who is being held here against his will."

The soldier blinked twice but didn't say anything.

"And it looks like he's being used for some sort of horrible experiment, as like human ammunition or something," Kiki said, "because we just saw him get shot out of a cannon and land in that tree over there."

I guess Lester felt like he had to chime in and say something, because he added, "Cool gun you got there."

The soldier frowned as she stared hard at each of us, one at a time. Over her shoulder, the sun had risen behind a hill on the other side of the building, near where Arnold was still, as far as we knew, sitting way up high in a tree.

"I've seen some crazy stuff in my day," she said, mostly to herself I think, "but this is right up there."

We waited for her to decide what to do. It was possible she would laugh at us, or yell at us, or even put handcuffs on us. But she did none of those things. Instead, she motioned for us to walk alongside her.

"I know your father," the soldier told me. "Colonel Brantley is a good man. I guess you're a lot like him, huh?"

A warm feeling filled my chest. "I guess," I said, trying not to sound too proud.

She spoke quietly into some sort of walkie-talkie, then turned back to us. "My name is Sergeant Kelly," she said. "I'd like you all to come with me."

"Where are you taking us?" Lester asked. "Are you taking us to Arnold?"

The soldier chuckled softly. "You want to hear something funny?" she asked. Then, without waiting for an answer, she said, "I thought Norbus Clacknozzle was a tough name. But Arnold Z. Ombee might even be worse."

TOGETHER—SATURDAY, 7:13 A.M.

Arnold

I looked down from the top of the tree and saw the three small shapes moving off the riverbank and toward the building and Dr. Grasmere.

"FOUR MINUTES LEFT, NORBUS!" Dr. Grasmere yelled up through his megaphone. "FOUR MINUTES LEFT TO JUMP DOWN! AFTER THAT, WE WILL HAVE NO WAY TO REACH YOU EXCEPT TO ATTEMPT A VERY DANGEROUS HELICOPTER RESCUE." He paused for a second, then added, "WE HAVE CALLED THE KINDERS. THEY ARE ON THEIR WAY. THEY HAVE ASKED ME TO TELL YOU TO PLEASE BE SAFE AND TO JUMP DOWN WHILE YOU STILL CAN."

If I had four minutes left to jump, that meant I had three minutes and fifty-nine seconds to decide. I didn't want to stay in the Territory. I wanted to make new memories, to replace the old ones that were blurry and fragmented. I wanted to go back to my old new life.

"I WILL JUMP DOWN IF I CAN GO HOME!" I yelled. "I DON'T WANT TO STAY HERE!"

But no one was paying attention to me, because they couldn't hear me, of course. I was two hundred feet up in a tree. Instead, I could see Dr. Grasmere turn his attention to the three humans who had emerged from the river. He talked to them for about a minute, then picked up the megaphone.

"NORBUS, THERE ARE SOME PEOPLE HERE WHO WOULD LIKE TO TALK TO YOU. YOU HAVE THREE MINUTES LEFT."

I saw the red jacket moving, and I realized Dr. Grasmere was motioning to one of the smaller humans. As the human walked toward Dr. Grasmere, I noticed it was limping slightly. I thought I recognized that limp. And then, a split second before the human started talking, a new memory flashed through my brain, and I knew exactly who it was.

The blood in my body got so warm, for a second it felt like I was an actual person.

"ARNOLD? IT'S ME, EVAN. I'M HERE WITH KIKI AND LESTER. SARAH ANNE AND DARLENE ARE WAITING BACK AT THE CAR. WE ALL CAME TO SAVE YOU."

I couldn't believe what I was hearing.

"SO ANYWAY, CAN YOU DO ME A FAVOR AND COME DOWN BEFORE THEY ARREST US?"

Evan

I handed the megaphone back to the man in the red jacket. "Thank you."

"You're welcome," he said. "Now go back over there and wait with your friends."

I walked back to Kiki and Lester. "Nice job," Kiki said.

Lester shrugged. "I might have thrown in something about how we're kind of total heroes, but that's cool."

The man in the red jacket lifted the megaphone to his mouth. "TWO MINUTES, NORBUS."

Sergeant Kelly, who was next to us making sure we didn't do anything stupid like try to climb the tree Arnold was in (as *if*), leaned down. "I've gotten to know your friend a little bit over the last few weeks," she said to us. "He's a good kid. I could tell he was a little different. I guess I didn't know *how* different."

"Of course he's different," I told her. "He's a zombie."

The sergeant shook her head. "I mean, even for

a zombie. Most of them do exactly what they're pro-grammed to do. But your pal? It seems like he's got a mind of his own."

"You mean, like a regular person," Kiki said.

Sergeant Kelly nodded. "Yeah, I guess I do."

Suddenly, there was a rustling in the branches high above.

"ONE MINUTE!" yelled the man with the mega-phone. "IT'S NOW OR NEVER, NORBUS!"

Kiki scowled. "I wish he'd stop calling him that," she said.

Arnold

I stood on the branch. My feet were trembling a little bit. I had another sudden memory: I was surrounded by human children, in a gymnasium somewhere, and I was trying to walk across a thin piece of wood. But I kept falling. I couldn't jump five feet onto a soft blue mat without getting scared.

This time, I needed to jump two hundred feet onto a parking lot.

"YOU CAN DO IT, ARNOLD!" yelled the female human girl into the megaphone.

Maybe she was right.

And it felt good to be called Arnold again.

I closed my eyes and jumped.

I felt the wind blow back my hair as I plummeted to the ground. And then the strangest thing happening: As I was falling, all the memories opened wide, opened all the way, and I could remember my whole life outside—my family, my friends, my school, even the bed I didn't sleep in in my bedroom.

It was all there.

I opened my eyes just in time to see the pavement rushing up toward me. I closed my eyes again.

And I stuck the landing.

HELLO AGAIN

So yeah, like I said, I stuck the landing. The next thing I knew, there I was, standing right in front of Dr. Grasmere. Next to him was Sergeant Kelly, and next to them, soaking wet, were the three shapes I'd seen from the sky.

"You're Lester," I said. "My brother. And you two are my friends Evan and Kiki."

The three of them looked at me, blinking. Finally Lester said, "That's right, we are."

Remember I told you zombies can't cry? That doesn't mean we can't be incredibly moved by the generosity and courage of our friends and family.

"Did you come here for me?"

"Yes," Evan said, his voice choking a little bit. "And we're so glad you're okay."

Kiki's eyes were shining. "Can I tell you something? It was Sarah Anne's idea."

I nodded. "That I can believe."

Lester has this word he loves to use—*chill*. I think it means *look like you don't really care about anything*. And at that moment, he was definitely trying to look chill. "So yeah," Lester said. "We just thought, you know, that we'd come here and take you home. We didn't realize that you'd be, like, hanging out at the top of a giant tree when we got here."

"That was strange and unusual," I said. "Even for me."

Before we could get any further in the conversation, though, Dr. Grasmere stepped between us. He turned to my three rescuers. "I hope you all realize that what you've done is a federal crime," he said. "You could all be in deep, deep trouble."

I pulled on Dr. Grasmere's arm. "Please don't do anything to them!"

"That's yet to be decided." He signaled to all the soldiers. "I need everyone to return to their stations, immediately."

But no one moved.

"Did you not hear me?" Dr. Grasmere said, his voice sounding strained. "Please get in your vehicles and go!"

But still, not a soul budged.

I saw a bead of sweat pop out on Dr. Grasmere's

forehead. "I don't understand. AM I SPEAKING A FOREIGN LANGUAGE?"

At that, Sergeant Kelly stepped up. "No, sir, you are not. But we have received orders from another party to stay put."

Dr. Grasmere's face darkened in confusion. "Another party? And who might that be?"

Right at that moment, a giant SUV rolled up next to us, and Regional Commander Jensen got out. Next to him was a man I recognized, with sudden shock, as Evan's father—former Regional Commander Horace Brantley.

Evan's eyes went buggy. "Dad? What—where—how did you find me?"

"I told you I would take care of it," Mr. Brantley told his son. His voice was stern but his eyes were kind. "However, it appears you have the same desire to get things done as I do."

Evan beamed proudly.

"We'll discuss this further when we get home," Mr. Brantley said, and Evan's beam dimmed a bit.

Regional Commander Jensen glared at Dr. Grasmere, who stepped back meekly. "I will take it from here," said Commander Jensen. He turned to me. "Son, it's come to my attention that you were returned here under false pretenses."

"False *what*?" Evan whispered.

"Someone lied," Kiki whispered back.

Commander Jensen turned back to Dr. Grasmere. "I'm not sure if you're aware, but Colonel Brantley and I have worked together for many years, in various capacities. He was my mentor, my boss, and we have a great deal of trust between each other. So, when he came to me and explained the situation, I could not let it stand." His eyes bored in on Dr. Grasmere. "Is it true? Did you tell the Kinder family that you were bringing the subject back here simply to have him train the other subjects for integration into society?"

Dr. Grasmere's eyes fell in shame. "It was the only way to ensure the subject's return," he said, his voice barely above a whisper.

"He wanted me to spy on the Kinders!" I blurted out. Dr. Grasmere went white, and I realized that Commander Jensen didn't know about that part. Dr. Grasmere was doing that on his own.

The commander's eyes narrowed. "I see."

"It—it was in the early stages," stammered Dr. Grasmere. "As soon as we were confident in our progress, you would have been informed immediately."

"ENOUGH!" barked the commander. He glanced around and spoke loudly enough so that all could hear. "Our work here is important, very important. But not so important that we do it under duplicitous circumstances."

"Duplicitous?" Evan whispered.

"Beats me," Kiki whispered back.

"Dr. Grasmere, you are relieved of your duties, effective immediately."

Dr. Grasmere looked stricken. "But—"

"IMMEDIATELY," pronounced Commander Jensen, in a tone of voice that made Dr. Grasmere realize he'd better keep his mouth shut before any more bad news came his way. Still, he couldn't help but mutter, "It was the only way."

Commander Jensen looked at me again. "As for the rest of us, let's return to the orientation building, to meet Dr. and Mr. Kinder. They will be here in a few minutes, and we can all discuss next steps." The commander turned to Kiki. "Your parents have also been notified."

Kiki looked calm. "I'm not worried. My parents knew exactly what I was doing," she said.

I stared at her, shocked. "Really?" I whispered.

She winked at me. "Of course not."

good-BYE FOR NOW

Twenty minutes later, I was sitting in a conference room, when my parents walked in. At least, I *hoped* they were *still* my parents. In any event, I'm going to start calling them Mom and Dad again.

My mom ran over to me and wrapped me up in her warm arms. "Oh, Arnold!" she said, at least six times. Then she moved on to "Are you okay?" which she said around three times.

"I'm fine," I said, twice.

My dad was quiet, but the power of his hug said more than a thousand words could have.

Commander Jensen stood up. "There is no real need to go over all the details of what happened right now; there will be plenty of time for that later. What is important is for you to know that everyone is safe," he continued. "Norbus has expressed his desire to return to your care, and we have decided to grant him permission to do so."

Lester leaned over and high-fived me, which hurt a tiny bit.

My mom looked like she'd seen a ghost—the friendly kind. "Really?"

Evan's dad smiled. "Yes, really."

"I'm afraid that certain representatives of the government have not been totally honest with you—or with me, for that matter," said the commander. "Yes, we wanted Norbus returned to campus. We have been retraining our afterlifes to serve our society in a military capacity, and to be frank, we had concerns that exposure to society would render that impossible. We needed to study Norbus to learn more. We were not convinced that any reanimation subject could survive and thrive after exposure to human contact." He paused to take a sip of water. "Our team has done a great deal of work, and we have studied Arnold a great deal. We put him in some adversarial positions, and challenged him in many ways. We even tried to realign his loyalties, which briefly yielded results." He opened a folder, but his was yellow, not red. "In fact, you will recall that after one round of extensive memory realignment, he renounced his desire to return to human society and expressed a wish to stay here."

"Of course I recall," said my mother, with a hint of bitterness in her voice.

Commander Jensen went on. "I know that was hard for you. But you will be pleased to know that those feelings didn't last. For the first time ever, a reanimation subject was able to withstand our cerebral stress tests—"

Kiki raised her hand. "Is that just another way of saying brainwashing?"

The commander raised his eyebrow at her but did not respond to her directly. "As I was saying, for the first time ever, a reanimation subject was able to withstand our cerebral stress tests and . . . well, and think for himself. Which is, in itself, a major breakthrough for our program."

My mom frowned. "What does that mean?"

"It means that we've learned one very important piece of information—instead of our subjects not being able to survive after being exposed to regular society, they in fact thrive under those conditions. Dr. Grasmere wanted to use that information for nefarious purposes, but that plan stops here."

"Nefarious?" I whispered to Kiki.

"No clue," she whispered back.

Commander Jensen looked at my parents kindly.

"Dr. and Mr. Kinder, you are getting your wish. Arnold may return to your family, and Project Z as we know it will cease to exist." He paused, took a deep breath, and closed his folder. "And it is time to announce our findings to the public. We will continue to work with our other subjects here at Government Territory 278 in hopes that they, too, may someday be candidates for integration into society— provided they can be placed with families as loving as yours, of course."

My parents sat back in their chairs, with looks of great relief washing across their faces. As for myself, though, I had a single concern.

"So Azalea will be staying here?"

"Yes, she will," said Commander Jensen. "She is a member of the community. The only one who gets to leave right now is you."

"I see." I stood up from my chair. "May I say good-bye to her?"

Commander Jensen shook his head. "I'm sorry, I don't think that's best. All the subjects have been returned to their pods, resting before today's activities. There has been enough commotion for one day."

I hesitated, trying to decide what to do.

"Mom, may I borrow your phone?"

She looked confused for a second but handed me her phone.

And then, for the second time in twelve hours, I ran.

I ran all the way back to my pod, followed by Commander Jensen and Colonel Brantley, my parents and brother, Evan and Kiki, Sergeant Kelly, and about five other staff members. But I didn't care.

When I got to the pod, Berstus, Frumpus, and Azalea were lying down on their benches. They all immediately stood up.

"Hey," I said. "I just—I wanted to say good-bye. For now."

Azalea looked at me sadly. "In a month, you won't remember me," she said. "You won't remember any of this. And neither will I."

I shook my head. "We will. This time, we will." I took out the phone and handed it to Evan. "Will you take a picture of us?" I went and stood next to Azalea as he took the picture. Then I hugged Azalea. "It was great getting to know you. And I'll see you ... out there ... before you know it."

"Do you really think so?"

"I know so."

Azalea smiled. "Good."

I hugged Berstus and Frumpus good-bye, then turned to go. At the pod door, I turned back.

"Someone once said a really smart thing to me. Do you guys want to hear it?"

They all peered up at me. "Of course we do," said Berstus.

I smiled. "Zombies are people, too."

ONE LAST SHOCK

First we met Simon at his van and picked up Darlene and Sarah Anne, who wanted to come with us. Then we all piled into my parents' truck—the very same truck that had rescued me all those months ago—and drove home.

It was loud.

I told them everything—about the buzzing sounds and the red lights, about The Strength, about the time Dr. Grasmere tried to get me to Salt Melt my friend Azalea, and all the other ways they tried to turn me back into a zombie.

And then Kiki, Evan, and Lester told me all about wanting to come rescue me, and Sarah Anne coming up with this amazing plan, and not telling their parents, and getting up at four in the morning, and swimming across the river, and not believing their eyes when they saw me at the top of the tree.

Believe it or not, it all sounded pretty hilarious when you thought about it.

Sarah Anne was quiet the whole way, mostly looking out the window. I'm not sure she liked a lot of noise or commotion. At the end of the ride, I turned to her.

"Are you okay?" I asked.

She nodded, then reached for her board at last.

I'M GLAD YOU'RE BACK, she said.

Two days later, I went back to school.

The morning was fun. Mrs. Huggle hugged me, Nurse Raposo made sure I was okay, Coach Hank yelled at me, and four kids asked me for help with their homework. It was pretty much business as usual.

Then came lunch.

I had my bowl of jelly beans and was looking for a seat, when Ross Klepsaw and Brett Dorfman corralled me by the arm and steered me toward their table.

"How was it?" Ross said. "Were you, like, back with all the other freakos?"

"It was intense," I told them. "There was some brains eating, and some eye gouging, and a lot of dancing."

Ross and Brett squinted their eyes for a second,

actually considering whether I was telling the truth or not, before Brett smacked me on the back. "HA!" he yelped. "That's so not what happened!"

"Okay, fine," I said, "but what really happened is a government secret, and if I told you, I'd have to put you in jail for treason."

"Whoa," Brett said, eyes widening. "That'd be bad. Forget it, man."

Ross gave me a conspiratorial tug on my sleeve. "So, can we, like, get back to that thing I was telling you about?"

"What thing is that?"

Ross looked crushed. "Come on, you remember!"

I didn't have the energy to explain how all my memories were a little frazzled at the moment, so instead, I said, "Oh, right . . ."

"So what's your advice? What's the best way to get Kiki to like me? How did *you* do it?"

Oh, *riiiight*. Some tiny corner of my brain remembered that he'd asked me that, but it seemed like a lifetime ago. In any event, I had an easy answer to his last question.

"Act more like a freako," I said.

After a few more minutes, I extracted myself from Ross and Brett and joined Kiki, Evan, and Sarah Anne at a table in the corner. They were eating quietly, almost like all the excitement of the last week had drained their energy.

I couldn't blame them.

"Hey, guys," I said.

No one said anything, which was a little weird, no matter how exhausted they were. Something was up.

"What?" I said. "What's going on? Is something wrong?"

"Something's *very* wrong," Evan said. "Kiki just gave us some horrible news."

"Oh no," I said. I couldn't believe it. After all we'd been through, all the craziness and the courage and chaos, something was wrong? I had visions of everything starting all over again. "Is Dr. Grasmere back? Does he want to take me away again? Is it all over? Kiki, are you in trouble for coming to rescue me? Are you moving away? What's going on??"

They all shook their heads. "No, no, no, no, no and nothing," Kiki said softly. But it wasn't until Sarah Anne actually smiled a little bit that I knew it wasn't anything like that.

Instead, it was something even *more* shocking.

Evan sighed heavily, like he was about to tell me the world was ending. Instead, he said, "Kiki just told us that she thinks she likes Ross Klepsaw."

My eyes felt like they shot out of my head. I looked over at Ross, who was still at his table, happily snorting a piece of spaghetti through his nose.

"Are you serious?" I said to Kiki. "You actually like . . . *HIM*?"

Kiki shrugged. "Yeah," she said, sounding slightly embarrassed. "I wish I didn't, but I think I do. Isn't it awful?"

All I could do was shake my head.

"Humans are so weird," I said.

ACKNOWLEdgmENTS

Authors are people, too! But we're people who need A LOT of help when it comes to making books and getting books into the hands of actual readers (who are also people). I would like to thank Anna Bloom, Robin Hoffman, Lisa Bourne, Kelli Boyer, and all the amazing people at Scholastic and Scholastic Book Fairs and Clubs who do this work so brilliantly and joyfully.

aBout the author

© Suzanne Sheridan

TOMMY GREENWALD is the author of many books for children, including the CrimeBiters! series, the Charlie Joe Jackson series, and the football novel *Game Changer*. This is his first series for zombies.

PROJECT Z CONTINUES!

THERE'S A NEW ZOMBIE IN TOWN.

Azalea, Arnold's closest friend from the Territory,
is living with Evan's family and ready to try out
human elementary school. But is Bernard
J. Frumpstein Elementary School ready for her?

READ ON FOR A SNEAK PEEK . . .

THE FRENCH FRY GAME

Lunch was the worst.

The rest of the day wasn't so bad, but *lunch*—that time of day where every kid is basically saying to the world, "These are my people, and they're who I will be spending my precious hard-earned downtime with, during a brutal day of learning and reading and writing"—was really hard.

Because I had to sit there, watching Kiki and Ross giggle and gawk and make googly-eyes at each other, and pretend that I didn't care.

Actually, I should say *we* had to sit there, because my friend Evan was right next to me.

Don't get me wrong, though. It's not like I liked Kiki— and by like, I mean *like*. No, that wasn't it at all. I'm pretty sure us zombies don't think in terms of that kind of like. But I was still trying to accept the fact that one of the first and best human friends I ever made was now in what could theoretically be called a "romantic" relationship with the one boy who tormented me more than any other human during my early days at Bernard J. Frumpstein Elementary School.

(Sorry. I tend to use big words when I'm upset. I promise to never use the word "theoretically" again. Or "romantic," for that matter. Instead, I'll use something more age-appropriate. Like "squishy.")

So yes, I suppose I was a little unhappy about the whole Kiki–Ross situation. But it's not like I lost sleep over it—and not just because I don't sleep. I cared, but not *that much*.

But Evan, on the other hand . . . Evan was a different story.

He was taking it much harder than I was. I think maybe because he did, in fact, feel some of those squishy feelings about Kiki. Not that he would ever admit it, of course.

We were sitting at lunch one day, and it was the same old story. Everyone was enjoying their sandwiches (some kids) or pizza slices (most kids) or fish sticks (a few kids) or tofu salad (Evan) or jelly beans (me) or whatever it was they were eating, and chatting and laughing and occasionally throwing stuff and generally acting like fifth graders.

Except for me and Evan. We were acting like grouchy old men.

Ross, Kiki, and a few other kids were playing a game they called "How many french fries can you balance on your nose?" Ross was the reigning champion. This particular day, he was up to seven, which, when you think about it, is pretty impressive. No one else had managed to pile on more than four.

And then, all of a sudden, Kiki got hot. Somehow, she managed to stack up the fries so high, you couldn't even see her eyes. And not one french fry fell! None of us had ever seen anything like it. Even I managed to emerge from my general glumness to marvel at her accomplishment.

"Evan, look," I said, nudging his elbow. "Kiki's on a roll!"

"I don't care," he said, refusing to take his eyes from his food. "Piling french fries on your nose is so dumb. I mean, like, what is this, kindergarten?"

It didn't seem like the right time to remind Evan that we had all played a very similar pile-food-on-your-face game at his birthday last year.

But hold on.

It *did* seem like the right time to remind Evan that his birthday was coming up again pretty soon!

"Hey Evan, isn't your birthday coming up again pretty soon?"

"I guess," he mumbled. "But I'm not having a party this year."

"Seriously? Why not?"

"Because I don't feel like it." Then, without another word, he got up, put his tray away, and left the cafeteria.

Oh, boy. This was worse than I thought.

I wandered over to the french fry table to watch the end of the competition. It turns out that Kiki's stack had reached a grand total of fourteen french fries, a record that was sure to stand until the end of time. Or was it? Because Ross, who disliked losing almost as much as he disliked zombies—at least until he got to know them—wasn't about to give up.

"Last round!" crowed Kiki, reveling in her sure victory.

Ross did some body stretches, as if it were an athletic contest. "Oh, I got this," he said. "There's not a doubt in my mind, you're going down." He grabbed the plate of fries, tipped his head back, and motioned to his friend Brett to start placing the French fries on his nose. The gathering crowd, which now included most of the sixth grade, started chanting along with each fry. Even the teachers and lunch workers craned their necks to see what was going on.

"Four! Five! Six! Seven!"

I glanced over toward the cafeteria exit and happened to see Evan, who hadn't quite left after all. He'd poked his head back in, wanting to see how it ended, just like the rest of us.

"Nine! Ten! Eleven!"

And then—in the blink of an eye, exactly the way most momentous world events happen—the french fries all came tumbling down, off Ross's nose, back on to the tray with a soggy plop (they were quite damp and kind of gross by then).

The contest was over. Kiki had dethroned the reigning champ.

She thrust her arms in the air as the crowd's chant turned to "Kiki! Kiki! Kiki! Kiki!" Ross bowed before the new champion. "Congratulations," he said. "It couldn't have happened to a nicer person."

And then, from one second to the next, Ross kissed Kiki right on the cheek. And Kiki kissed him back! Right there in front of everyone!

Well, technically, not in front of *everyone*.

Evan had disappeared.

Again.

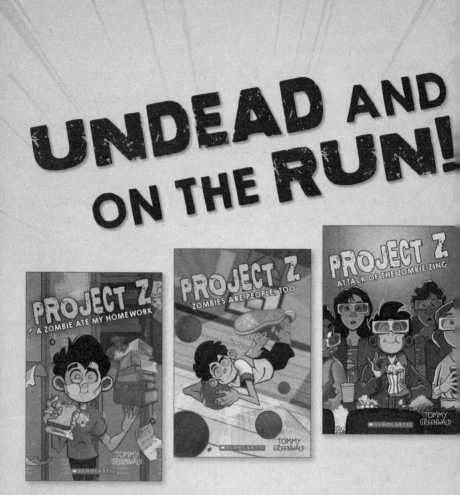

UNDEAD AND ON THE RUN!

A zombie kid faces the ultimate test: making it through human elementary school.

SCHOLASTIC
scholastic.com

GREENWALD